CARJACKED LAWYER (A TRAVEL NIGHTMARE)

By Donald W. Desaulniers

CARJACKED LAWYER (A TRAVEL NIGHTMARE)

Copyright 2022, Donald W. Desaulniers

PAPERBACK ISBN: 978-1-989683-42-2

TABLE OF CONTENTS

CHAPTER 1 (Wasted Career)

As I read this morning's newspaper, my attention was immediately directed to a name I recognized.

One of my law school classmates had just been selected to head up a state task force on white collar crime. The article even spewed out Carl's compensation which was to be $329,000 for the one-year period during which the task force was expected to operate.

That lofty sum seemed to me to be a prime example of white collar crime.

I'd been working as an attorney for the South Dakota state government in Pierre ever since I became a lawyer in 1992 and I was only earning $87,000.

By the way, my name is William Swanson but everyone calls me Billy. I'll hit age fifty-five next month which I believe means that I'll no longer be considered middle-aged.

My career has been remarkable only in its utter boredom.

I'm considered moderately proficient in drafting complex wording for various statutes, especially those related to financial matters.

As a result of that rather obscure talent, I've been stuck in pretty much the same job for the entire thirty years I've been employed.

In fact I haven't yet worked my way up to a corner office or even a workspace with a window.

Instead I've been hidden away in the same backroom cubbyhole for the entire time.

The office manager hasn't even assigned a secretary to me. The statutes I help draft are considered so complicated that the boss only trusts me to type them up since I'm the only one who would be capable of spotting an error in the wording.

I'm confident that all that disrespect will soon change. Finally both the office manager and my immediate boss have retired. Their joint going-away party was last week and we're all expecting their replacements to show up today which is Monday, the 29th of August, 2022.

In a few minutes I'll finish my breakfast and walk to work since my apartment is only a few blocks away from the office building where I'm employed.

Already I'm trying to determine which wall decorations to hang in my new office.

Despite being stuck in what turned out to be a dead-end job, I actually led a very happy life until four years ago when my wife Debbie died suddenly of a brain aneurism while she was working out at her health club.

Even though we had no children, Debbie and I were exceptionally compatible. Her career also in the state government was just as unfulfilling as my own, so we enhanced our leisure time with many enjoyable pastimes such as duplicate bridge and volunteering for various local charities.

Debbie was an avid gardener and our home in Pierre was beautifully landscaped.

Debbie's early demise absolutely crushed me and I've been something of a hermit ever since. I gave up all of the extracurricular activities we used to do together and now I spend my non-work time reading voraciously or watching television.

Since I had absolutely no green thumb, I sold our home last December including the furniture and since then I've been residing in a one-bedroom furnished apartment within walking distance of the government building where I'm employed.

It was a sunny and pleasant day so I didn't bother bringing an umbrella.

I hit the office precisely at nine o'clock, a skill I'd honed to perfection over the decades. It was important to me not to lose a minute of my personal time to the state.

A colleague accosted me and mentioned that our new bosses were scheduled to arrive at ten o'clock.

CHAPTER 2 (Forced Retirement)

Our division comprised about twenty employees. I was the only attorney. The other workers were liaisons with politicians and corporations throughout the state providing input regarding enforcement of statutory provisions. Most of the other folks in the office had their own secretarial support staff.

Shortly after ten o'clock the new arrivals waltzed in.

My jaw gaped open.

Both new arrivals introduced themselves and informed us that a few changes would be forthcoming.

The office manager was a young woman named Linda Marner who didn't appear to be more than twenty-five years old and my new immediate boss was even younger although I was unable to determine if it was male or female. Its name was Tracey Sawyer which didn't help with the mystery. The voice was also useless as a clue to the sex of my new boss.

I'd need to solve the puzzle before I addressed Tracey as sir or ma'am. Choosing the wrong door would not be conducive to making a positive first impression.

Their statements about imminent changes pleased me because it was about time that as the lawyer in the office, I was treated with more respect. In addition to a bright cheery office, I also hoped that a raise in salary would be forthcoming as part of the welcome new changes which would directly affect me.

We were instructed to return to our workspaces and informed that Linda and Tracey would be around to speak with each of us personally over the course of the day.

In fact it seemed that I was going to be rewarded by the new bosses because they came in to see me first. Seniority had some clout after all.

Linda Marner took control of our initial meeting.

"Good morning, Billy. Tracey and I have been examining the personnel records for the past few days so that we could hit the ground running today when we officially began our oversight of this office. I understand that you're the resident expert on legislative drafting."

"That's correct. I've been crafting the wording for many of the government's proposed statutes for my entire thirty year career."

"Are you proficient with the legal software which has been designed to prepare the new laws?"

"I don't use any software although I've taken a careful look at the programs. I deemed them to be vastly inferior to my own tried and true manual method."

I noticed both young bosses rolling their eyes at my comment. Suddenly I realized that I wasn't going to get a raise and an office with a window after all.

Ms. Marner continued.

"I've also noted that you're eligible for retirement because you've completed thirty years of loyal service to the government."

"That's true."

"Given that fortuitous circumstance, I've taken the liberty of declaring your position redundant."

"What do you mean?"

"Your job is being terminated."

"Are you firing me without notice?"

"That's not precisely accurate. We're providing you with an additional incentive to take a generous retirement package immediately. It's only if you choose not to formally retire that you'll get the push."

My jaw gaped open. These young idiots were booting me out of my legal career without even sitting down with me to learn in detail what benefits I brought to the legislative process.

Marner pulled some documents out of her briefcase.

"This sets out the terms you're being offered by the state government. Please read over the papers carefully. I'll need your formal response before the lunch break. In the meantime, Tracey will confiscate your government-issued smartphone and change your passwords for that device and for your office computer."

I was in utter shock.

Like the obedient serf I'd always been, I handed over my passwords and was then unceremoniously ushered out of my office and taken to a conference room by a security guard.

My legal career was now terminated and I was being treated like a thief.

The retirement package was satisfactory and I accepted the government's offer. My first payment would be made at the end of September.

My retirement would take effect today.

By noon I had signed the retirement documents and was escorted out of the building by the same security guard.

I walked home while carrying my personal effects in a small plastic carrying case.

My mind was mush on the short trek home.

CHAPTER 3 (Major Changes)

In the evening I was too distraught to go out for supper so I tossed some frozen burritos in the oven and washed them down with beer.

My personal smartphone never buzzed and nobody emailed me. I had half expected some of the office staff to call or email and sympathize with me over my abrupt departure. They knew my number.

Wryly I wondered if anyone even noticed that I had been booted out. There certainly wouldn't be any retirement celebration held for me.

It was like I'd never even worked there let alone devoted my entire career to the office.

I was decidedly morose when I crawled into bed at ten o'clock. Out of habit I set the alarm for seven o'clock the next morning.

After a few minutes of analyzing what had happened to me today, I reached over and shut the alarm off. There was no point in getting up early tomorrow.

My dreams in the night were confusing and I woke twice to go to the bathroom which gave me a few moments to recall the dreams. In both instances I was anxious because I was alone and adrift, firstly on some type of raft in the middle of a huge body of water, and then lost in a dense fog on a country road in the middle of nowhere.

Out of habit I woke up precisely at seven o'clock and couldn't get back to sleep.

What ensued was just about the longest day I had ever endured.

With no job to occupy my time, I wasted the entire day doing nothing except worry about how I was going to survive without my career to sustain me emotionally.

Wednesday was the last day of August and when I woke up that morning, I resolved to get a grip on my situation.

With that goal in mind, I spent the first part of the morning poring over my finances.

I had no debts whatsoever.

My bank accounts were quite flush with cash because of the great price I had snagged last year on my house sale. Although I had no separate retirement account, my state pension would bring in $50,000 per year until I reached age sixty-two at which point it would be reduced by the amount I would then begin to receive from social security.

My vehicle was an almost brand new 2022 Nissan Kicks which I had purchased this past April.

I certainly didn't need to snare another job. I could live most comfortably on my pension and savings.

By mid-morning I had decided that I was acutely embarrassed at having been summarily dismissed from my government legal career.

Running in to former co-workers or other acquaintances would be quite upsetting because Pierre was a small city and everyone in government knew the details of their fellow employees.

Debbie and I had never travelled. Her parents and siblings all lived near the small village of Avon about a hundred and twenty-five miles southeast of Pierre which meant that we spent virtually all of our vacation time visiting Debbie's family.

My own parents had died a couple of years before I met Debbie and I had no brothers or sisters. I had grown up in the tiny hamlet of Midland about forty miles southwest of Pierre.

I went to the superintendent's apartment in my building just before noon and inquired about vacating my unit.

As luck would have it, my timing was immaculate. A young woman had called just a few minutes earlier inquiring about immediate vacancies because she had to leave her own apartment by tonight and was desperate.

The superintendent called the girl back and she rushed over to view my unit.

To make a long story short, she loved my furnished apartment and we came to an arrangement whereby I would vacate immediately and the girl would move in while I was loading my belongings into my vehicle.

She paid the September rent.

Packing up my stuff took less than an hour and suddenly I was free as a bird with nothing holding me back from leaving Pierre.

I had no land line phone so I used my personal smartphone to cancel my TV cable and the new tenant agreed to hold onto any mail which happened to arrive. She would email me whenever something came in and I could contact her at that time. I rarely received any snail mail because I did most of my business online.

Utilities were included in my monthly rent.

I dropped into my bank and gave them instructions not to mail anything to me. I also withdrew ample cash and made a prepayment on my credit card.

Several years ago I had purchased at a yard sale a complete set of USA road maps. In the parking lot of my bank I sorted through those maps and picked out the ones for South Dakota and the

adjoining states. I also had a map
showing the entire USA.

By one o'clock I was ready to leave
Pierre.

Before I left town I drove past the
office building where I had spent the
past thirty years and gave the place
the middle finger salute.

CHAPTER 4 (Lawyer on the Loose)

The unexpected flurry of activity over the past couple of days had suddenly turned Billy Swanson into some sort of aimless tumbleweed.

I had absolutely no idea where I should go.

Pierre was in the dead center of South Dakota.

There hadn't even been time to decide how extensive this unexpected driving excursion should be.

Since nasty weather would hit the northern states in another month or so, I decided to head north first.

With that initial decision duly made, I pointed the car north and began driving on Highway 83.

Two hours later I was entering North Dakota.

Incredibly, this was the very first time I'd ever been outside the state of South Dakota. I had attended public and high school in Midland and then university and law school in Pierre.

I had never excelled at sports which meant that I never had the opportunity to travel to other cities and states for tournaments or competitions.

Avon was the furthest south or east I'd ever been. Once in high school I did go west on a bus trip to see Mount Rushmore near Rapid City.

I continued driving until I reached Bismarck where I found a hotel room.

There was a diner next door to the hotel so I ate supper there. Back in my room, I began studying my collection of maps.

Since I was totally unvaccinated, I couldn't travel further north into Canada.

Montana was to the west but it was a vast and sparsely populated state which really held no scenic interest for me.

Spending the day alone in my car had been reasonably fulfilling today because I'd been excited to see so much new territory and enter a state I'd never before visited.

I wondered if I'd begin to feel lonely as the driving trip progressed.

After much indecision, I finally decided to head east tomorrow morning and see a bit of Minnesota.

A continental breakfast was included in my room rate so on Thursday morning I ate in the hotel lobby before hitting the road.

Today was the first day of September.

I began the drive on Interstate 94 but quickly decided that I preferred smaller highways so at Dawson I caught

Highway 3 south until it intersected with Highway 13.

At Wahpeton I crossed the Bois de Sioux River into Minnesota. By then it had begun to rain which sucked all the joy out of driving.

The local news on my car radio indicated that the storm only encompassed the central and northern portions of Minnesota so I caught Highway 75 south and followed it to Pipestone where I got another hotel room.

Although the rain had stopped about an hour south of Wahpeton, the skies were still cloudy for the remainder of the day.

Disappointingly, I discovered that I really wasn't enjoying being cooped up in my vehicle all day.

I had purchased a submarine sandwich when I filled up with gas at Pipestone before locating this hotel, and I ate my sub up in my room.

Again I pulled out my maps but this time I was too discouraged to plot out another long day's drive.

I decided to drive south into the extreme northwest corner of Iowa and then spend tomorrow night in Sioux Falls which was the largest city in South Dakota and a place I'd always wanted to visit.

My main conclusion was that being a retired lawyer on the loose wasn't my cup of tea.

CHAPTER 5 (Depressing Thoughts)

I woke early on Friday morning and
checked out of the hotel. I found a
diner on my way out of town and stopped
to eat a full breakfast.

In order to add another state onto
my list, I continued driving south on
Highway 75 until I'd entered the
extreme northwest corner of Iowa.

When I reached Highway 9, I turned
west and drove into Sioux Falls.

I stopped at a park and walked
around in order to get a good look at
the falls and then I located the
Pettigrew Museum and wandered inside
that stately old mansion for a while.

Sioux Falls was a rather large city
and frankly I didn't feel entirely
comfortable with the traffic.

After I finished touring the museum,
I sat in my car and tried to decide
whether to get a hotel in the city for
tonight or continue with my driving
trip.

I looked over the South Dakota map
and decided that I was close enough to
Nebraska to drive through a small
section of that state.

Opting to leave Sioux Falls
immediately, I found small Highway 42
which I followed west out of the city.

When I reached the intersection of Highway 81 twenty minutes later, I headed south and crossed the Missouri River at Yankton into Nebraska.

I then caught Highway 12 west. I had intended to stop at Avon and perhaps visit Debbie's elderly parents but then I recalled that her sister had informed me last Christmas when I'd phoned that her Mom and Dad were both in a nursing home suffering from dementia.

Some depressing thoughts began to slither into my mind.

It struck me that my entire legal career had been wasted.

Rather than using my education to help folks with their legal problems, instead I had gravitated immediately upon graduation into the stable world of government service.

Crafting the wording for various statutes didn't help anyone. In fact it was unlikely that my work made even the slightest difference to anything.

Only a tiny fraction of legal cases ever dove so far into the weeds that the precise wording of a particular clause turned out to be crucial in the outcome.

An even more frightening thought occurred to me.

With no close friends or family, how on earth was I going to cope with unlimited free time?

My original plan to kill a few months by exploring America had already turned out to be a huge disappointment.

Being cooped up in my vehicle all day was tough on my legs and back. By late afternoon my legs began to cramp up and my back, neck and eyes were sore.

At least I had seen four new states.

But already I was tired of driving.

It was time to decide on a tentative small town in which to live out at least the next few months or years of my boring existence.

One tiny advantage to remaining in South Dakota would be that I wouldn't have to change my vehicle licence plate.

Besides, that was the only state in which I was authorized to be an attorney.

Perhaps setting up my own small law office would provide me with the opportunity to dredge up a bit of self-worth. At the moment I felt like a complete and utter failure.

I pulled off to the side of the road and examined the South Dakota road map.

Highway 183 was a few miles up ahead. If I drove north on it then I would reach the small city of Winner.

That seemed like a fitting name for a loser like Billy Swanson.

CHAPTER 6 (Abandoning South Dakota)

I pulled in to the city of Winner at four o'clock while wondering if the start of the Labor Day long weekend was a terrible time to be looking for a hotel room.

The chain hotels were fully booked but I spotted a private motel and they had a vacancy for tonight only so I took it. I'd worry about tomorrow night's accommodation tomorrow.

The motel had Wi-Fi so I checked out apartment rentals and home prices on the internet.

That endeavor caused me to question what I really wanted for my future.

Opening up my own legal practice was a foolhardy idea. For one thing, I wouldn't know a soul in Winner which meant that dredging up clients would be very difficult.

Another drawback was that I had forgotten everything I'd ever learned about family law, real estate law, criminal law and virtually every other type of work that a small town attorney would need to be familiar with in order to adequately serve the clients.

From the internet I also discovered that there were already loads of lawyers in Winner. Even though it was the county seat of Tripp County, the place had less than 3,000 residents.

Trying to start a law office here would be nothing but a drain on my pocketbook and on my confidence level which was already scraping the bottom of the barrel because of my abrupt expulsion from my job.

I walked around the downtown area which was rather uninspiring. The landscape was extremely flat.

By the time I'd finished supper at a diner near my motel, I had made my decision.

Winner was not the right location for my new life.

That epiphany led to a renewed desire to see America after all despite the lukewarm experience of my driving trip over the past three days.

In the evening I studied maps and that activity rekindled my excitement over the next phase of my travel adventure.

I slept soundly and on Saturday morning I checked out of the motel and drove west on Highway 18.

I gassed up in Hot Springs just before noon and continued driving on the same highway.

Half an hour later I entered the state of Wyoming and veered south.

When I eventually reached Cheyenne, I found a hotel for the night.

The drive today had been invigorating, perhaps because my mental attitude had improved so drastically.

For the first time since losing my job, I had felt free of stress and responsibility.

The uncertainty of my future now excited me rather than filling me with worry.

I wondered if I'd ever bother to return to my home state of South Dakota.

CHAPTER 7 (Avoiding Storms)

On Sunday morning I checked out of my hotel right after breakfast and ten minutes later found myself in the state of Colorado.

A Greeley radio station began giving warnings about a wicked band of late summer rainstorms ravaging the mountain areas from Denver and Pueblo all the way west to the Utah border. Those storms were also dumping major snow in many of the higher elevations.

The weather east of Interstate 25 was cloudy but free of storms.

I drove east about fifty miles to Fort Morgan where I caught smaller Highway 71 and followed it south until the highway ended at the intersection of Highway 350 on which I drove southwest to Trinidad.

By then it was just starting to rain lightly so I decided to call it a day and found a hotel room.

This hotel had its own small diner so I ate my supper without needing to go back out into the rain.

The TV weather indicated that nasty storms were going to ravage the western half of New Mexico over the next several days.

That dampened any enthusiasm I had to head over any mountain ranges. I hauled out my road maps and decided to amend my trip route significantly. Rather than see the southwestern states this time around, I opted instead to head east where the weather was expected to remain pleasant.

Monday was the Labor Day holiday.

I ate breakfast in the hotel diner and then continued my journey.

My day's drive began on Interstate 25 which I followed south for a few miles until I entered New Mexico at which point I caught small Highway 64 east.

Ninety minutes later I stopped for gas at Clayton and glanced again at my maps.

By staying on Highway 64 I could take in a bit of the Oklahoma Panhandle before veering south into Texas.

At Guymon I stopped for a light late lunch and a bit later caught Highway 83 which I followed south into the Texas Panhandle.

The scenery was quite different from what I had experienced so far on the driving trip.

By the time I reached the small city of Childress, I was sick of driving and found a motel for the night.

I purchased a submarine sandwich and bottle of Pepsi when I filled up with gas on the outskirts of Childress and I ate in my motel room.

As I studied my Texas state map, I decided that the one highlight I definitely wanted to see was the Riverwalk in San Antonio.

I had heard of the series of canals meandering through a portion of that city and one of my well-travelled colleagues at work had commented that the Riverwalk was by far the most interesting place she had ever visited.

San Antonio was about 425 miles south of Childress and I decided to head there tomorrow.

After seeing the city, I would likely drive east into Louisiana and visit the Gulf States despite the fact that hurricane season was in full swing.

CHAPTER 8 (Glorious City)

Tuesday morning was cloudy and as a result I slept in until nine-thirty because no sun was streaming in through the curtains.

Since I was hungry, I ate a late breakfast at a nearby diner before hitting the road.

The rain began by the time I reached Paducah and that slowed my progress.

By the time I made it to Fredericksburg, it was already five o'clock and I was quite exhausted.

Rather than hit San Antonio in the evening, I found a hotel in Fredericksburg and ate supper in the hotel's main dining-room.

The weather for this portion of Texas was supposed to be sunny and warm tomorrow and I was hugely anticipating my visit to San Antonio.

As the weather station had promised, Wednesday morning was bright and cheery.

About an hour after I got my early start, I arrived at the outskirts of San Antonio.

By following the directions on an inset map of the city, I located the Alamo first and took a tour of that historic building.

Then I drove to the Riverwalk area and found a municipal parking lot for my vehicle.

I'd never been so excited as I strolled around the shops and restaurants lining the narrow canals.

In fact I stopped at a couple of the boutique hotels along the way and booked a room at one of them for tonight even though the nightly rate of $175 was quite expensive. My Nissan could be left overnight in the municipal lot. I walked back to my vehicle and brought a small carry-on bag back to my hotel, and I also prepaid the parking charges.

For the rest of the day I amused myself by taking a couple of cruises on small boats along the canals and generally just walking around admiring the beauty and quaintness of this touristy section of San Antonio.

I was in a marvelous mood. This city was by far the highlight of my driving adventure so far.

In fact I was having such a fantastic time that I booked the hotel room for tomorrow night.

For my supper I ate in a lovely little bistro at an outdoor table overlooking the canal.

At dusk I decided that San Antonio was a huge city and that I'd best retire to my hotel room for the night.

On Thursday morning I woke quite refreshed. Doing so little driving yesterday had been a great change and today I likely wouldn't even use my car although I would definitely check on it and pay the parking fee until tomorrow at noon.

Whereas yesterday had been pure joy, reality settled in shortly after I finished breakfast.

On my way to the municipal parking lot, I was accosted by several panhandlers, a couple of whom were quite aggressive.

I prepaid my parking charges and returned to my hotel where I chatted with the desk clerk.

He informed me that Texas was facing a massive homeless problem mostly caused by drug addictions and waves of illegal immigrants which had been crossing into the USA from Mexico in record numbers ever since Joe Biden had become president.

Apparently yesterday either I simply hadn't noticed any bums or I'd been fortunate to avoid them.

Whatever the reason, the deadbeats were out in full force today and that kept me inside my hotel room studying maps for the remainder of the day.

For supper I ate indoors at the closest restaurant to my hotel and scurried back to my room well before dusk.

At least I'd seen the famous Riverwalk and enjoyed its ambiance.

CHAPTER 9 (Difficult Drive)

On Friday morning I slept in and ate a late breakfast in the same diner where I'd eaten supper last evening.

Today I fully expected to drive east out of Texas and spend tonight somewhere in Louisiana.

After checking out of my hotel, I walked briskly to the municipal lot and managed to avoid several panhandlers by crossing the street a couple of times.

Thankfully my vehicle was undamaged and I began my trek eastward at eleven o'clock.

It was about 200 miles to Houston and another hundred to the Louisiana border, a reasonable drive for the day.

The weather was cooperating.

I started out on Interstate 10 but at Seguin I decided to get off the freeway and take much smaller Alternate Highway 90.

That decision proved unwise as I encountered flooding and a detour at the hamlet of Sublime.

That slowed me down considerably just as it began to rain rather heavily.

Some of the bridges were reduced to one lane which meant long waits until the eastbound traffic was permitted to proceed.

I cursed myself for not remaining on Interstate 10.

In fact I was making lousy time and finding today's drive to be a real ordeal.

I stopped at motels in Rosenberg and Richmond but learned that most accommodation had been conscripted by the various levels of government to temporarily house illegal immigrants.

Apparently finding a hotel or motel room in Houston would be much easier because of the vast supply. Houston was the fourth largest city by population in the USA.

Dusk had fallen by the time I made it to the western outskirts of Houston, and I was a bundle of nerves.

It made sense to attempt to traverse the main portion of the city and find a hotel room on the east side of Houston.

Unfortunately a traffic accident forced me and other motorists off Alternate Highway 90.

Although I tried to follow the traffic, I wound up totally lost in a massive metropolis at night.

Eventually I reached a commercial street where hopefully I could stop at a business and ask for directions to take me to Interstate 10.

Various concerns began to haunt me.

For one thing, my South Dakota licence plate targeted me as a lost tourist.

The few folks I happened to see walking on the sidewalks in the rain were all people of color. I was an old White guy who would appear to be an easy robbery target.

It was possible that this was a Spanish speaking section of Houston in which I couldn't even obtain understandable directions.

My gas gauge was approaching the red line which was another area of worry. I should have stopped for gas earlier but I had been fixated on finding a motel and hadn't noticed that my fuel was getting low.

It was again raining quite hard.

Finally I spotted some neon lights up ahead.

As I got closer, I was relieved to realize that a gas station was coming up. There were only two gas pumps and both were occupied so I backed my vehicle into an empty spot at the far end of the parking lot in order to wait for one of the gas pumps to be free.

CHAPTER 10 (Carjacked Lawyer)

In case it was necessary to prepay for the fuel, I turned off the ignition, undid my seatbelt, opened the car door and began to step out of the Nissan with the intention of running through the rain into the small store and prepaying for my gas while at the same time getting proper directions to Interstate 10.

I hadn't quite made it out of the car when strong arms suddenly grabbed a hold of me.

I let out a startled cry and found myself staring into the face of a tattooed thug. The interior lights of my vehicle illuminated my assailant's face clearly.

With increasing horror I also saw that a second thug was standing immediately behind the guy who had grabbed me. He was even scarier than the young man who had me in his grasp.

I let out a shout for help but all that earned me was a crushing fist into my face.

It was impossible to fight back. The next thing I knew I had been dragged onto the ground and one of the thieves had closed the door.

We were engulfed in darkness. There were no overhead lights in this far section of the parking lot.

The two men were talking in a foreign language I assumed was probably Spanish.

Rough hands rifled through the pockets of my pants and the scary thought filled my mind that these low-lifes were going to steal my wallet containing most of my identification and all of my cash.

Billy Swanson was suddenly going to be stranded in Houston with nothing but the clothes on his back.

I fervently wished that I had avoided this dangerous city but it was far too late now to change my route.

It was raining quite hard and I realized that my shouts for help would never be heard in the storm.

This was the first dangerous situation I'd ever encountered.

Conventional wisdom I'd recalled from various police shows reminded me not to fight back. Let the thugs rob me and probably steal my Nissan. Fighting back was not only futile but doing so might well get me killed.

Not content merely to rob me, the two men began hitting and kicking me. I caught my breath and shouted again for help.

That's the last thing I remembered as suddenly I felt something heavy clunk against my head. I blacked out.

If I had been conscious and capable of seeing in the dark, I would have watched the two thieves drag me around to the rear of the building where they removed my wedding band and felt around for my watch.

They were out of luck in that regard because I hadn't worn a watch in many years.

The men also removed my shoes.

I would also have seen the men return to my Nissan, start it up with my key fob and drive off with the second robber following my vehicle in a beat-up old car.

Had I also been able to feel, I would have realized that I had wet my pants at the front and fully released the contents of my bowels into the seat of my trousers.

Billy Swanson had been the latest victim of a violent car-jacking.

CHAPTER 11 (Dead Addict)

The rain continued until three o'clock on Saturday morning.

Billy Swanson lay unconscious in his own excrement behind the gas station.

The station had closed up at midnight.

On Saturday morning the owner arrived in the darkness at six-thirty to open up his business.

His assistant showed up late shortly after nine o'clock, much to the annoyance of Juan Gonzalez. It was so difficult to find and retain reliable employees.

In the early afternoon, Gonzalez told Arturo to take the garbage out to the dumpster behind the station.

A few minutes later Arturo returned breathlessly and informed Juan that there was a dead drug addict out back.

Arturo was busy with a customer and couldn't even be bothered to check out the corpse. When he had rung up the purchases and the customer had left the store, Arturo dialled 911 to report the dead body.

The dispatcher took down the address and advised that the police would be notified and that Arturo shouldn't disturb the body in any manner.

Three hours later a squad car pulled into the station and Juan instructed Arturo to show the cop where the body was.

When the deputy bent over to examine the corpse, he almost gagged at the stench. Dead drug addicts were popping up like weeds throughout Houston. The open southern border had become an unfettered pipeline for powerful illegal drugs.

The deputy called for a non-emergency paramedic van to cart away the smelly deceased gentleman. He warned the service that the corpse would need to be hosed off first because of the filthy state of the body.

It only took twenty minutes for the van to arrive.

The attendant's assistant wore gloves and a plastic shield face mask as she hosed off the corpse and removed the soiled clothing.

The smelly clothes were disposed of in a sealed plastic container after which the two attendants moved the naked body onto a gurney for transport to their vehicle.

"There are no needle tracks or other evidence of drug use. Are you certain that this fellow is a homeless drug addict?"

"He sure smelled like one and that's how the owner of the gas bar described him when he called it in."

At that point the deputy received a call from dispatch and roared off in his vehicle to handle the emergency.

The attendant placed his hand on the back of the deceased.

"Rigor mortis hasn't set in yet. In fact the body isn't all that cold. I wonder if the sun warmed up the corpse before we got here."

"Maybe we should check the guy for signs of life," the assistant suggested.

The attendant attempted to feel the gentleman's wrist and neck for a pulse but was unsuccessful.

"Let's get him inside the vehicle. It's too windy out here for me to detect any sign of life even if the chap was still in the land of the living."

Since this was a non-emergency transport vehicle only, it contained no sophisticated equipment.

The attendant tried again to detect a pulse or any other sign of life but was unsuccessful.

They proceeded to one of the nearby hospitals in order to drop off the corpse and obtain their next assignment.

CHAPTER 12 (Total Neglect)

The attendants wheeled their gurney into the hospital and directly to the morgue area where they were instructed to place the corpse on a moveable metal table and then to place a sheet over the body.

The attendants did as instructed, filled out a bit of paperwork and departed.

Billy Swanson remained out of sight under the sheet for the next twenty-six hours before finally an orderly was instructed to bring the corpse to one of the examining tables.

No autopsy had been ordered but the hospital administrator had requested a cursory examination of the homeless gentleman so that at least a preliminary cause of death could be attributed.

The sheet was pulled off the body and old Dr. Brian Hadley bent down to take a better look at this inert slab of white meat.

Hadley had actually retired as the Chief Medical Examiner eight years earlier at age seventy-four, but the hospital had implored him to return part-time in the fall of 2020 to assist during the Covid-19 acute staff shortages.

Hadley briefly felt the corpse but was immediately puzzled.

He glanced at the accompanying paperwork and noted that the body had been brought by paramedics to the morgue at five o'clock on Saturday afternoon. It was now after seven on Sunday evening.

Something was amiss.

Hadley was old-school and knew precisely where best to check for a faint pulse.

He let out a startled gasp when he realized that the corpse he was about to carve into was in fact still alive.

"Carlos, this man isn't dead. Help me wheel him up to the emergency department."

They quickly pushed the moveable metal table out into the hallway, down to the elevator and then rode up to the main floor which housed the ER.

Hadley informed the intake clerk that the body had been languishing in the morgue for the past twenty-six hours and that a nasty lawsuit might be avoided by tending to the homeless gentleman immediately.

"We're too swamped to handle another indigent patient," the clerk complained.

"I'd strongly suggest that you make room. If you're lucky, he'll die anyway and no one will ever know how negligently he's been treated."

Reluctantly the clerk opened the doors to permit Hadley and the orderly to wheel this new patient into the actual Emergency Room.

Hadley corralled a young female doctor and explained what had occurred.

"I'll hook the gentleman up to a drip immediately but all the rooms are full. The poor guy will have to join the dozens of other patients in the corridors."

The unconscious man was transferred to a proper hospital cot at which point Hadley and his assistant wheeled their now empty metal table back to the morgue.

Hadley moaned to Carlos that the health care system was deteriorating at breakneck speed right before their eyes.

Dr. Karen Schmidt hooked this latest unwanted patient up to a drip and found an empty spot for him to rest far down the corridor. At least the patient would now receive life-sustaining liquids during his final hours.

Not a single medical person gave Billy Swanson another glance until late Monday afternoon when someone noticed that the drip was empty and needed to be refreshed.

Billy received no additional attention whatsoever until two o'clock on Tuesday morning when old Dr. Hadley popped in unexpectedly to discover whether the homeless man had died since being brought into the ER.

CHAPTER 13 (Talking Corpse)

Dr. Hadley had the intake clerk open the doors to the ER where he wandered up and down the corridors looking for the homeless bum since the clerk had confirmed that the John Doe he had brought in two days earlier was still listed as a patient.

Hadley finally spotted the man around a corner pretty much all by himself.

He read the chart which confirmed again that the medical system was collapsing. No medication except for the drip had been administered to this patient and no doctor had examined him in any manner since the poor chap had been admitted and given the first drip.

Since no one else was around, Hadley decided to examine the patient since he hadn't had the opportunity in the morgue.

There were no needle marks in either arm or in the abdomen area. In fact Hadley could see no evidence of substance abuse. The patient's teeth after a cursory look seemed to be well cared for.

Something didn't add up.

Many addicts with lucrative careers had discovered that an undetectable area for injections was in the upper thigh near the groin.

Hadley pulled the sheet away. The staff hadn't even bothered to put a hospital gown on the patient who was stark naked under the sheet.

The elderly doctor leaned down in order to closely examine the groin area.

...

My eyes fluttered open.

I was awash in confusion. Harsh light hurt my eyes and I had to squint in order to see anything without discomfort.

My head turned and I saw that I was hooked up to some plastic bag which indicated that I must be in a hospital.

Just then I felt something on my thigh.

I raised my head and saw that some sicko was bent over my groin and presumably just about to give me a blow job.

"Get those lips away from my genitals, pervert. You're not my type."

A white-haired old man gasped, stood erect and then burst out laughing.

"Welcome back to the land of the living," he joked. "I wasn't sexually molesting you. I'm Doctor Brian Hadley and I was merely checking your thigh area for signs of drug addiction."

"I don't do drugs. Why would you possibly think otherwise?"

"You were found lying in your own excrement behind a gas station a few days ago and you've been in a coma ever since. Everyone assumed you were a homeless addict. Do you have any idea what you were doing there?"

"I don't seem to recall much of anything."

"Do you know your name and whether you have any family?"

I thought for a moment but was unable to answer either question.

"You'd think I'd be aware of my own name but I'm coming up blank."

"You must have suffered a concussion which has affected your memory. Do you have any aches and pains?"

"I'm sore all over and my throat is parched."

"I'll find someone to bring you water. I may not be able to locate a doctor. It's the middle of the night."

"You told me you were a doctor."

"I'm actually a retired coroner."

"Why were you examining me? I'm not dead."

"Funny you should mention that. In fact everyone thought you were dead. You were laid out on a metal table in the morgue and I was just about to cut you open to determine how you died. Your body wasn't cold and rigor mortis hadn't set in so I checked you for a pulse and determined that you weren't dead after all. That was the first time in over forty years that one of my deceased patients turned out to be still alive."

The coroner excused himself while he ran off to find me some water.

CHAPTER 14 (Amnesia Sucks)

To say that I was confused was a gross understatement. Somehow I had no memories whatsoever. At the moment I was a complete mystery to myself and apparently to everybody else.

Suddenly I realized that I badly needed to pee.

The coroner hadn't returned yet.

With great difficulty I began to ease myself off the cot until it dawned on me that I was stark naked.

The urge to pee overcame my modesty and I sat up, managed to stand on the floor and then wrapped the sheet around myself. It appeared that I'd already had a minor urinary discharge because the sheet bore at least two modestly sized yellow stains.

I had no idea how to disengage myself from the contraption hooked up to my wrist, but I certainly didn't want to drag the drip equipment around while I searched for a bathroom.

After examining the hook-up for a moment, I figured out how it worked and freed my wrist from the two tubes.

Then I slowly walked down the hallway until I found a bathroom.

I was too weak to stand at the urinal so I sat in one of the stalls. Peeing was incredibly pleasurable.

When I had finished, I went to the sink and gazed at myself in the mirror.

It was a complete stranger staring back at me. There wasn't even a hint of recognition. I did look like a tramp. My face was covered in what looked like several days of stubble. That told me that whiskers grew even when we were in a coma.

I washed my face and felt a lump on the side of my head. That area was very tender to the touch. I also had some bruising on one side of my face and a black eye. I wondered if I had been beaten up.

I cupped my hand and drank a bit of water from the tap.

The tiles were cold on my bare feet.

I left the bathroom and wandered back to my cot. There was still no sign of the coroner or anyone else although I passed many other cots along the corridor. Every patient I passed was sound asleep assuming they were all still alive.

I climbed back onto the cot in an attempt to warm my feet.

The coroner returned a few minutes later with a bottle of water and some hospital employee.

I swigged some of the water. The coroner assured me that this woman would look after me and then he indicated that he had to return to the morgue and get back to work. I thanked him for his concern about my well-being.

The lady was not very pleasant.

"We need to determine immediately whether you have medical insurance. If you're indigent, then we're extremely limited in the level of care we can provide to you."

"Somehow I doubt that I'm broke and homeless, but unfortunately at the moment I have no recollection about anything, not even my own name."

"That's unacceptable."

"Perhaps you could take my fingerprints and determine my identity from them."

"This isn't the police department. We're not equipped to obtain and check fingerprints."

"I don't know what else to suggest."

"Other than your claim regarding memory loss, your chart doesn't indicate that you require any medical attention. I'm going to recommend that you be released into a local homeless shelter. This hospital doesn't have the resources to house you until such time as your memory returns."

"If you do that, I'll at least need some clothes. I don't mean to gross you out, but I'm completely naked under this sheet."

The woman's lip curled up in disgust.

"I'll see what can be done to clothe you and send you on your way."

I was too weak and confused to argue with the woman who marched off with a scowl on her face.

I leaned down to the end of the cot and took my chart off the clipboard. It was somewhat puzzling. Paramedics had been summoned by the police to the rear of a gas station at 1711 Sinclair Street. They couldn't detect any signs of life but I was wallowing in my own excrement so they hosed me off, removed and disposed of my clothing and then apparently brought me directly to the morgue on Sunday the 11th which coincidentally was the anniversary of the 9/11 attacks in 2001. I wondered why I knew that piece of information but was completely blank about myself.

I was identified on the chart as Patient John Doe 629. I couldn't tell from the chart whether that designation was created by the paramedics, the morgue or the hospital.

Dr. Hadley had begun his examination of me more than a full day later and that's when he realized that I was still alive. It appeared that he and an assistant wheeled me over to the Emergency Room and that I had languished on this cot ever since.

The only medical attention I had received was to be hooked up to the saline drip which was replenished once before I woke up a short time ago.

I don't understand why I did it, but I folded up the single page of paper which constituted my medical chart. I intended to keep my own chart. It appeared to be the only chronological evidence of what had happened to me.

Having no known identity definitely made me both a pest and a financial burden on the system.

Somehow I couldn't make myself believe that I was some variety of deadbeat. That just didn't feel right.

CHAPTER 15 (Pest Eviction)

I closed my eyes and drifted off to sleep.

The next thing I knew I was being shaken awake.

A security guard hovered over me.

"Wake up, sir. The hospital has rounded up some items of clothing for you. Please follow me. Your discharge papers have to be signed before we release you to the care of a shelter."

I felt a lot better after the sleep. I put my folded medical record into my left hand and followed the guard on foot while the soiled sheet was wrapped around me like a toga.

I saw on a wall clock that it was now eight-thirty. It was light outside so that indicated that it was still Tuesday morning.

It didn't seem proper to be kicked out of the hospital when I still didn't know my ass from two dollars a week, but my mind was too fuzzy to complain or even comprehend precisely what was happening to me.

We arrived at the waiting area of an administration office of some sort where I was handed a sports bag and told to get dressed. The guard stepped out of the office while I examined the selection of clothing, every item of which was obviously well used.

Nothing except the socks and running shoes fit me properly but at least I was now fully clothed.

There was no electric razor in the sports bag but it did contain a toothbrush, a tiny tube of toothpaste and a change of underwear and socks.

Apparently this would constitute my net worth until I was somehow able to sort myself out.

The hospital clerk who processed my release instructed me where to sign the paper.

I read over the form and realized immediately that in it I was waiving all rights to sue the hospital for any reason relating to my medical care.

"I'm not signing this form. The coroner told me that you fools didn't even have the basic competence to make sure that I wasn't still alive before dumping me in your morgue. That smells like gross negligence to me as does booting me out of this place when I can't even remember my name."

My mini-rant got the attention of the clerk who asked me to wait while she contacted her supervisor.

An older lady arrived a few minutes later but she was rude and condescending.

In the end I still refused to sign the release form. The woman handed me a street map of this section of Houston along with a bus token. She had circled the location of the homeless shelter which was expecting me. At that point she summoned a security guard who escorted me out of the hospital.

Once the guard had gone back inside, I weighed my options.

Before heading to the homeless shelter, I decided to go back inside the hospital and find the morgue so that I could thank the old coroner for assisting me and complain to him about being tossed out on the street with no memory.

Although I had to ask directions a couple of times, I located the morgue and knocked on the locked door.

A young woman opened the door after a few moments and asked me what I wanted.

"I'd like to speak with Dr. Hadley if he's still here."

"His shift ended at six o'clock."

"Is there some way for me to contact him?"

"I'm afraid not, sir but I can leave him a message."

"That won't be necessary, miss."

I went back outside.

It was a shame that Hadley wasn't in the hospital because so far he'd been the one and only person who appeared to give a shit about my welfare.

The homeless shelter was less than a mile away and the weather was warm and sunny, so I decided to walk there rather than use my bus token. I felt like I needed some exercise to clear the cobwebs from my brain and loosen up my joints and muscles.

It struck me that I was damn hungry but the hospital hadn't fed me and I had no money. Perhaps the fools expected me to eat the bus token.

CHAPTER 16 (Legal Assistance)

As I walked toward the shelter, I
happened to pass a lawyer's office
sign.

Something struck a chord with me
that my situation called for an
attorney in order to eradicate the
hospital's smug and uncaring attitude.

I definitely needed some help.

The office was up a steep set of
stairs at the side of a somewhat run-
down building which didn't infuse me
with confidence but this could be the
only legal office I'd pass on my way to
the homeless shelter.

I trudged up the stairs, rather
pleased with my physical stamina since
I'd been unconscious and presumably in
pretty rough shape for several days.

The sign on the door at the top of
the stairs was for James B. Corbett,
Attorney-at-Law.

I knocked, opened the door and
stepped inside.

Nothing about this office emitted
even the tiniest hint of success.

The room contained a beat-up old
wooden desk and a few ratty chairs.

In fact I suddenly lost my
confidence and started to leave when a

voice from an inner office boomed, "I'm open. How can I assist you?"

A grey-haired man in shorts and a golf shirt emerged from the other room, sized me up in an instant and a look of dejection filled his face.

"I'm sorry but I don't hand out money to panhandlers. There's a homeless shelter about half a mile west of here. They might be able to help you."

"Actually that's where I'm headed but I happened to notice your law office sign and thought I might speak with you about my situation."

"I take it that you're broke."

"That's very perceptive of you. I never wear my Rolex on Tuesday. I won't waste your time after all. I can see how swamped you are with paying clients."

I turned to leave but the lawyer stopped me in my tracks with his own snarky retort.

"You've got a sarcastic mouth for someone in your pathetic circumstances."

"Let's just say that I've had a lousy day and my social niceties have gone on strike."

"As you rudely noted, I'm not busy right now. Why did you want to see an attorney?"

"I'm contemplating suing the hospital a few blocks east of here."

"Why is that?"

"I've got my hospital chart with me. The creeps just evicted me from their facility and referred me to the homeless shelter. It seems that the medical system has treated me like shit from the moment they found me and I strongly believe that I'm not well enough to fend for myself."

"What's your name?"

"I don't know. I've got amnesia."

"Do you really expect me to believe that line of bullshit?"

"It would be foolish for me to believe that a highly successful lawyer like you would take a client's word for anything. I'm sure you didn't make it to the pinnacle of your profession by trusting any fellow human beings."

"For a deadbeat you're unusually feisty."

"Everyone I've met since I regained consciousness has immediately assumed that I'm a homeless tramp."

"Don't blame me for that. You look like a bum."

"The hospital provided me with these clothes which all look like they fished them out of a dumpster. My unshaven appearance and facial bruising certainly don't make me look like I just stepped off the cover of a fashion magazine, but I just can't believe that I'm any sort of transient or deadbeat."

"What do you know about yourself?"

"I have no knowledge whatsoever about myself. Apparently nobody has been attempting to find me. The only limited information I have about my situation is set out on my medical chart. You can look at it if you want before you make up your mind whether to kick me out of here."

"I guess I can do that, but I need to make it clear that you are not my client."

"That's fair enough."

CHAPTER 17 (Surprising Result)

I handed Mr. Corbett my medical chart after extracting it from my pocket and unfolding it.

He sat on the edge of the big desk in this waiting room and began perusing the document.

"It says here that you were found behind some gas station lying in your own feces."

"I'm shocked. You can actually read."

Corbett continued reading.

"This is incredible. The medical examiner says that he was just about to carve you up in order to ascertain the probable cause of death when he realized that you weren't even dead."

"Did you note the sentence in which Dr. Hadley confirms that I was lying in the morgue on the metal table with a sheet over my entire body for more than twenty-six hours?"

"Your situation is getting more and more interesting."

"By that comment I assume that the dollar signs are beginning to swirl around in your head."

"You're obviously not quite as stupid as you look. Since you don't even know your name, what do you want me to call you?"

"You may as well call me John Doe 629."

"Do you have any idea what you want me to do for you besides threatening the hospital and the paramedic company with a lawsuit?"

"I don't feel that I should have been released from hospital and told to go to a homeless shelter. I'd like to be readmitted. Surely they don't expect someone in my condition to regain his memory all on his own."

"I fully agree. Did the hospital provide you with a business card of a person to contact?"

"The only things they gave me were these ratty clothes and a boot in the ass on my way out the door."

"I'll take your case on a contingency basis which means that I'll receive forty percent of any money I manage to squeeze out of anybody."

"You're not worth forty percent. Don't be so greedy. I'm the guy who has been treated negligently, not you."

"You drive a hard bargain for someone with no assets."

"As I already said, I doubt if I'm indigent although I can't figure out why my family isn't looking for me."

"What makes you think you've even got a family?"

"I just don't feel that I've lived alone for my entire life."

"What percentage of any settlement would you feel comfortable tossing my way?"

"By the looks of you and this dumpy office, I guess you could use the money every bit as badly as I could. I'll agree to a contingency legal fee of twenty-five percent."

"That's excessively low."

"If I had any confidence that you weren't a completely useless boob, then I'd be inclined to be more generous, but right now your inspiration quotient with me sits at near zero."

"Since you put it so nicely, I'll accept twenty-five percent. Come into my inner office and I'll bang off a retainer agreement before I contact the hospital."

I sat in a chair across from Corbett while he prepared and printed off the retainer document.

He handed it to me along with a pen and pointed out where I needed to sign.

"I need to read it first," I snarled.

The wording was acceptable but one anomaly leapt out at me.

"Is this your own form or is it a precedent you've used?"

"It's a standard form recommended by the state bar association."

"They've done a lousy job of creating it."

"What do you mean?"

"Clause 7(c) refers to a previous Section 5(b)(ii) but that section doesn't even apply. They meant to refer to Section 5(b) (iv) but whoever drew up the original form was sloppy."

"I've been using that form for several years. I'm sure you don't have a clue what you're talking about."

Corbett grabbed the form and read the applicable clauses.

"You're actually correct. How on earth did you spot that?"

"I have no idea but I'll sign the form if we both initial the change I pointed out."

"It's a deal, John Doe 629."

We both signed the document and then Corbett picked up his phone and called the hospital administration office.

Surprisingly the shyster was quite persuasive and by the time he had spoken with someone in authority, the hospital had agreed to readmit me immediately.

Corbett put a sign on his office door that he'd return at one o'clock and he drove me to the hospital and waited while I was duly admitted. He even coerced them into giving me a private room with a phone.

Corbett followed me up to my room so that he would know how to reach me. Then he left in order to contact the hospital's legal department as well as the paramedic service.

I thanked Corbett for his work and joked that perhaps I had jumped the gun in branding him as incompetent. However, a bit later the thought came to me that someone like me who had amnesia probably didn't possess the mental capacity to understand what he was signing. Likely I'd be able to get the agreement nullified on that basis. Apparently that legality hadn't entered Corbett's addled brain or possibly he was so desperate for work that he decided to risk it.

CHAPTER 18 (My First Dream)

The afternoon was taken up with various medical tests after I had been served a rather late lunch.

The hospital was giving me the royal treatment now that they realized that a lawsuit was a strong possibility. Presumably they were anxious to mitigate the damages and minimize any claim against them.

Supper was quite tasty.

A young woman named Dr. Augustin arrived in my room shortly after I'd finished my meal.

"We have some good news, sir. Although there's a bit of bruising in a small portion of your brain, no bleeding or serious damage was detected by the various pieces of equipment you were subjected to today."

"Do you have any idea when my memory might return?"

"My boss examined your results personally and he indicated that the most likely scenario is that your memory will return in a matter of days."

"That's a relief because right now I can't recall a single detail about my life. The biggest puzzle for me is why nobody appears to be looking for me."

"You don't speak with a Texas drawl so perhaps you're not from Texas."

I raised the fingerprint issue and Dr. Agustin said that she would make inquiries on my behalf.

"Another puzzle for hospital administration is your financial status. You speak like a highly educated gentleman and that suggests that you are neither homeless nor indigent."

"I look forward to learning the truth about myself. It is quite disconcerting having a blank memory."

The doctor left.

I was not hooked up to any monitoring or medical devices.

Finally the staggering events of the day caught up with me and I fell asleep.

Many hours later I was jolted awake after a vivid dream.

A pretty woman was walking hand in hand with me down a lovely country path. I didn't speak but the woman said that she wanted to visit her parents on the weekend which meant that I wasn't to book any weekend appointments with my clients.

I relived the dream over and over in my mind and deduced that I was probably an accountant or a lawyer although I couldn't figure out why the woman wasn't out there looking for me. I had the sense that the lady was my wife even though the few words she spoke hadn't mentioned that we were married.

Eventually I fell back to sleep but couldn't recall any other dreams when I woke up much later as sunshine was streaming in my hospital room window.

That dream was the very first indication that I had an actual past history.

Breakfast was delivered and I was just sipping the last of my orange juice when I had an epiphany.

The woman in my dream was Debbie Bronson. That must also be my surname.

Doctor Agustin dropped in a bit later to check on me and I excitedly told her about my dream. She indicated that my brain was probably in the process of recalibrating my memories and gushed that the dream was a very positive sign.

CHAPTER 19 (Memories Return)

Over the next few days my dreams became more frequent and I was able to gradually piece together bits of my past life even though the dreams were too fragmented to ferret out my identity.

The miracle occurred as soon as I had woken up on Monday, the 19th of September.

My mind had returned with a vengeance and I recalled everything.

The reason why nobody was searching for me was because Debbie had died four years earlier and we had no children.

I phoned James Corbett who answered his own telephone.

"I'm back in the land of the living, Corbett. All my memories have come back. My name is Billy Swanson and I'm a recently retired government lawyer from South Dakota. The reason no one is searching for me is because I'm a widower and we had no children. I was carjacked at that gas station in Houston by two thugs."

"I'll contact the police on your behalf, Billy and I'll come to the hospital whenever they advise that they can attend there to take down your victim statement. Welcome back."

"While I'm waiting for you and the cops, I'm going to contact my credit card company and my bank. The carjackers must have relieved me of my wallet, my smartphone and my wedding ring as well as my vehicle."

One of the staff provided me with the emergency number for my credit card as well as for my bank.

I contacted the bank first. Fortunately no cash withdrawals had been made from any of my accounts. The same held true with my credit card. I had refused to allow the flash and tap feature to be added to my card because I was old-fashioned and didn't trust modern technology. That actually protected me because the thieves thereby couldn't utilize my card since they didn't know my password.

I also called my insurance company to report the theft of my vehicle and explained why it had taken me ten days to contact them.

Next I contacted my smartphone service provider. They checked my phone and concluded that it must have been destroyed by the thieves once they had determined that they couldn't use it without knowing my password.

Corbett called me. The police would send a detective around to the hospital tomorrow morning to take my statement. Corbett had a small claims court trial tomorrow so wouldn't be able to attend at the hospital. I assured him that his presence wasn't required.

For the remainder of the day I spoke with a couple of doctors about my condition and thought at length about my life. It was fantastic having my memories back and knowing exactly who I was.

The hospital was thrilled to obtain my medical insurance details and I was informed that I'd likely be discharged tomorrow afternoon.

CHAPTER 20 (Police Work)

My insurance company had indicated that they would have a rental car and a hotel room ready for me tomorrow once I was discharged. They would also deliver today to my hospital room the sum of $500 in cash so that I could pay for taxis and meals until my new credit and bank cards were issued.

Similarly my bank had advised that they would issue a new bank card to me which I could pick up at a particular branch in this section of Houston tomorrow. My replacement credit card would also be ready at that bank branch.

The cash arrived in the afternoon. Having a bit of money gave me a feeling of again being in control of my own destiny.

On Tuesday morning at nine o'clock Detective Moe Enright arrived at my room and took my preliminary statement about the carjacking.

"Do you think that you'd recognize the carjackers?"

"Their faces are permanently engraved in my brain. I won't have any difficulty whatsoever in identifying them."

"Can you drop by my office after you're released from here? I'd like you to look through some mug shots of known local carjackers."

"I'd be happy to do so, Detective."

I was provided with a nice lunch after which a doctor arrived to sign my discharge papers.

Using the hospital room phone, I called the insurance adjuster looking after my file and she confirmed that the rental vehicle was already at the Quinte Hotel along with a replacement smartphone. The other items in my vehicle such as my clothing and personal effects were not insured because I had cancelled my apartment liability and contents insurance just before I left Pierre.

Since my vehicle was only seven months old, my policy provided me with full replacement coverage meaning that the insurance company would pay to purchase a brand new 2022 Nissan Kicks if one was available or a new 2023 model if no 2022's could be located at this late date in the model year.

After a bit of discussion, the adjuster agreed to inquire at some of the Houston Nissan dealerships and let me know if she located a replacement vehicle for me. She asked me to call her from my new smartphone to let her know my new phone number at which time she would let me know if she had been successful in locating a new car for me.

I took a cab to the Quinte Hotel and picked up my room key as well as the new smartphone and rental car key.

I activated my smartphone and then called the insurance adjuster to inform her that I had checked into the Quinte Hotel. She was still searching for a new car for me and would let me know once she had located one.

My next call was to James Corbett. We discussed a monetary sum which I'd be willing to accept in settlement of my negligence claims against the paramedic company and the hospital. Since I seemed to now be pretty much back to normal, I told Corbett that I'd accept $20,000.

I showered thoroughly before venturing back out. Rather than drive to the police station, I took a cab since I was very leery about big city traffic.

Detective Enright brought me into a small room in which he had collected several books containing mug shots of known carjackers. He left and said that he'd return in about thirty minutes to see if I recognized either of the criminals who had stolen my vehicle and assaulted me.

I was on the fourth album when I spotted the tattooed freak.

The second assailant was not in any of the twelve photo albums.

Enright returned and I pointed out the thief to him.

"Are you reasonably certain that this is one of the men who attacked you?"

"I'm absolutely certain."

"I'll pull up his file on the computer. Perhaps we can figure out who he habitually hangs out with and thereby identify the second attacker."

That endeavor proved successful.

The thug who had grabbed me was a career criminal named Jorge Estevan and his most frequent "known associate" was named Carlos Montoya.

Estevan had seven arrests for carjacking but only two convictions.

I identified Montoya's photo as the second attacker. He had convictions for theft and assault but none for carjacking.

Detective Enright had me describe the contents of my vehicle as well as my wallet and ring. I also provided him with the South Dakota licence plate number which was OXK459. Enright said that he would call my insurance adjuster to obtain the VIN number of my stolen vehicle although he cautioned that by now my Nissan had almost certainly been chopped up for parts by a chop-shop or was on its way to Africa or South America on some ship.

Enright assured me that he would keep me abreast of the investigation and thanked me for my cooperation.

CHAPTER 21 (Lawsuit Settlement)

My next stop by taxi was at the branch of my bank where my new bank card and credit card had been sent.

I activated both cards while at the branch and then grabbed a cab back to my hotel.

I called James Corbett and provided him with my new smartphone number.

He had spoken with the attorneys for the insurance companies representing both the hospital and the paramedic company. Corbett felt that everyone involved appeared to favor a quick settlement of the issue. A non-disclosure clause would be required since neither defendant wanted the extreme negative publicity that dissemination of the facts would entail.

Despite my aversion to driving in Houston, I took my rental car to a department store relatively near my hotel and purchased some clothing and toiletries including an electric razor.

While I was still in the parking lot, my smartphone buzzed. It was the insurance adjuster. She had found a 2023 brand new Nissan Kicks at a dealership in the small city of Barrett which was about twenty miles northeast of Houston. This vehicle was virtually identical to the one which had been stolen and contained a minimum of extras and computer features. Because of the lateness of the model year, no brand new 2022 Nissan Kicks could be located anywhere in this general area.

I agreed to accept ownership of the vehicle in full satisfaction of my claim and drove immediately to Barrett in order to take possession of my new car. The adjuster advised me that the dealership would look after returning my rental car to the agency.

This new Nissan was even the same black color as my previous vehicle. I signed the necessary paperwork and drove back to my hotel in my new car. It bore a Texas licence plate.

This was the first positive result arising out of my ordeal. I now owned a 2023 Nissan Kicks with zero mileage in place of my 2022 which because of the trip had racked up quite a lot of miles. That somewhat made up for the fact that the insurance company wasn't paying to replace my clothes and personal effects.

As far as my accommodation costs, the adjuster and I came to an arrangement whereby they would pay for my hotel for four nights in total after which I would look after all my own expenses. That meant that as of

Saturday I'd have to find my own hotel. This Hotel Quinte was $225 a night which was substantially above my price comfort level.

The adjuster also warned me that it was incredibly difficult to find an available room at any but the most expensive hotels. Illegal immigrants were being temporarily housed in motels and budget hotels all over Texas.

I ate supper in the hotel dining-room and adjourned to my room.

Exhaustion overtook me and I went to bed at eight o'clock.

Corbett called me shortly after I'd eaten my room service breakfast on Wednesday morning. He had already come to a tentative settlement agreement with the two insurance companies. The paramedic outfit would pay me $15,000 and the hospital would kick in another $45,000.

I was fully satisfied with those amounts even though Corbett warned me that if I suffered any subsequent trauma or other complications from the incident, I would be out of luck in obtaining any additional compensation.

We made an appointment for one o'clock at his office where I would sign the release forms reflecting the terms of settlement.

I was quite relieved. Even though I wanted the paramedics and the hospital to be spanked for their abysmal treatment of me, I had no desire to have a lawsuit hanging over my head for the next year or two.

There were no last-minute glitches in the negotiations and by mid-afternoon I was in possession of Corbett's trust check in the amount of $45,000 and he had earned an easy $15,000 for a few hours work.

We were both happy campers.

CHAPTER 22 (Police Line-Up)

I slept soundly on Wednesday night at the hotel.

On Thursday morning Detective Enright called.

The two suspects had just been arrested and a line-up had been arranged for one o'clock at his police station. I assured him that I'd be there.

I'd watched the occasional police show on TV in which similar looking suspects were lined up in order for an eye-witness to determine if the perpetrator was present. That was the very limited extent of my knowledge regarding police procedure.

Detective Enright led me into a room which contained a one-way mirror which enabled me to look through to the adjoining room in which the pending line-up was to take place. The men in the line-up would not be able to see into this room which meant that my identity would be kept private.

Six men were lined up and I saw both suspects immediately.

"Do you recognize any of these men as the ones who attacked you at the gas station?" Enright inquired.

"Yes I do. My two assailants were Numbers 2 and 5."

"Are you positive about that?"

"I'm absolutely certain. Number 5 dragged me out of my car and punched me while Number 2 stood behind him and grabbed me once I was fully outside my vehicle."

"Did you see them steal your Nissan Kicks automobile?"

"No I didn't. I was rendered unconscious within seconds of being attacked and the bastards left me for dead behind that gas station."

Enright picked up a phone on the wall and instructed the guards to detain Numbers 2 and 5 and allow the other gentlemen to leave.

Thereafter he called another number and informed the recipient of the call that Jorge Estevan and Carlos Montoya had been positively identified as the attackers.

Enright brought me in to a small conference room where he recorded my statement that I had identified Jorge Estevan and Carlos Montoya as my assailants.

While I was signing an affidavit confirming the results of the line-up, Enright received a phone call.

The detective informed me that a judge had just issued a search warrant for the apartment where both Estevan and Montoya resided.

I left the station and returned to my hotel.

Unfortunately I had very little confidence in the justice system but at least the two thugs had been arrested. Somehow I doubted if they would ever be convicted of any serious assault charge and likely wouldn't even be charged with theft of my vehicle since there was apparently no direct evidence that they had stolen my Nissan. I was certain that circumstantial evidence would never in this disgusting WOKE culture be sufficient to convict a person of color.

Two hours later Enright called me again and requested my presence at the police station immediately.

I drove there and received some positive news.

The two assailants had retained souvenirs of their numerous car thefts and assorted assaults.

My South Dakota vehicle licence plate was nailed up to their apartment wall along with dozens of other similar plates.

Also, an empty Gucci wallet with my initials engraved in one corner was also seized along with assorted rings and watches. My presence was required in order to ascertain if any of the seized loot belonged to me.

Perhaps Lady Justice wasn't out of the USA on an extended vacation after all.

CHAPTER 23 (Catch and Release)

When I arrived at the station, I was quite thrilled to identify both my wedding ring and my Gucci wallet.

There was absolutely no doubt that it was my wallet. The two idiots hadn't realized that some high-end wallets contained a secret compartment.

When I instructed Enright where the hidden spot was located, he pulled away the fake flap to reveal $200 of my cash along with one of my business cards from work which I had left in the wallet just in case I lost it and an honest person found it and would thereby have a means of contacting me.

All the other contents of my wallet had been removed and their whereabouts were unknown.

The wallet and ring had to be kept as evidence for the time being.

Additional charges of theft and carjacking would be laid against Estevan and Montoya based on the seized evidence and my affidavit that the items belonged to me.

I spent the rest of the day obtaining more maps from an American Automobile Association office since my own collection would almost certainly never be recovered. I also purchased a few more miscellaneous items from a department store and then examined my maps back in my hotel room.

Tomorrow night was the last night that the insurance company would cover my hotel cost. I surmised that I'd like to leave Houston on Saturday morning and continue with my driving excursion.

I'd definitely learned my lesson. From now on I would avoid all large cities. They were too dangerous for an old guy like me who was travelling on his own.

On Friday at noon I received a phone call from Detective Enright.

Estevan and Montoya had lawyered up and had both been released on their own recognizance earlier this morning.

I told Enright of my tentative plan to leave Texas on Saturday morning since the insurance company would not cover my accommodation expenses after Friday night.

He informed me that eventually I might have to return to Houston to testify against the carjackers but that the court system was so overwhelmed that it might be two years or more before their trials took place. Both men through their lawyers had already pled not guilty to all charges.

I had watched Fox News on my television most nights when I was in Pierre and recalled how many Democrat run states and cities had virtually banished bail for all but the most serious of crimes.

That policy had resulted in the same criminals being arrested and released time after time.

The two thugs who carjacked me certainly fit that profile. Enright had admitted that from the licence plate collection on the apartment walls of the two men, they were committing regular car thefts of one sort or another.

Wryly I wondered if they would steal another vehicle tonight in order to come up with some cash to pay their attorney. In fact I had mentioned that speculation to Detective Enright when he told me that the two guys had already been released.

CHAPTER 24 (Good Police Work)

Moe Enright ended the call with Billy Swanson and leaned back in his chair.

Swanson had joked about Estevan and Montoya stealing another vehicle in order to pay their attorney, but the possibility of that happening was actually quite substantial since a quantity of cash had also been seized at the men's apartment.

They would need to replenish their cash resources quickly and would almost certainly employ their tried and true method of stealing cars.

Enright called his supervisor and ran that theory by the woman. She authorized some clandestine temporary surveillance on Estevan who appeared to be the leader of the pair.

Officer Tommy Fleming was assigned the task and he took up a position near the old home in which the men rented an apartment. Their 2009 dark grey Chevrolet Malibu was parked at the building when Fleming arrived just after darkness had fallen.

Stakeout work was incredibly boring and generally garnered no positive results but tonight proved to be an exception.

Both Estevan and Montoya emerged from the building at nine-thirty and climbed into their vehicle.

Fleming followed them discreetly.

He watched as they stopped at a used car dealership and broke into the office using a glass cutter.

A few minutes later Fleming saw the lights of one of the cars in the lot flash on. Evidently the thieves had located the key fobs and had chosen which vehicle to steal.

One of the men climbed into the stolen SUV and drove away with the Malibu following close behind.

Fleming again followed the cars and called for backup.

The stolen vehicle was driven to a body repair shop on a street housing various seedy buildings, some occupied by businesses and others apparently vacant.

The Malibu parked outside the garage and the driver stepped out.

One of the repair bay doors opened up and the stolen SUV was driven right in while the other driver walked inside.

Two squad cars arrived within five minutes and the five officers in total duly announced their presence.

No one opened any of the doors so the police were forced to break the smallest of the doors in order to enter the premises. Again they announced themselves as police and ordered everyone to get down on the ground.

At this late evening hour, there were only two employees on site in the body shop.

Before being arrested for receiving stolen merchandise, one of the employees was allowed to call his boss and advise him about what had just occurred.

That supervisor arrived ten minutes later at which point the two employees in the body shop were arrested and taken into custody.

Estevan and Montoya were also arrested and charged with break and enter at the used car dealership and grand theft auto. They were also taken to the police station.

Two more police officers arrived and they began perusing the vehicles in the body shop looking for additional stolen merchandise.

In fact of the nine vehicles in the garage, two appeared to be owned by legitimate customers and the other seven were all very recently stolen.

The supervisor was permitted to lock up and secure the garage after the officers had completed their assessment of the vehicles.

A warrant was obtained authorizing the temporary closure of the body shop and the seizure of all computers and other financial records found on the premises relating to the business.

This appeared to be a rather large operation and would likely wind up solving a whole raft of auto thefts in Houston.

CHAPTER 25 (Victim Statement)

On Saturday morning I had breakfast in the hotel dining-room and then returned to my room to brush my teeth and use the toilet before checking out of the hotel and finally continuing my driving adventure.

My smartphone buzzed. It was Detective Enright informing me in great detail about last night's successful stakeout and requesting my presence on Monday morning at the bail hearing for Estevan and Montoya.

I reiterated my desire to leave Texas immediately and was adamant that I had no intention of paying $225 plus taxes to extend my stay at this hotel.

In the end I relented and we came to a compromise.

Enright had one of his staff call around and a room at a budget motel could be mine for the next two nights for $82.95 per night including tax.

I checked out of this luxury hotel and drove to my new temporary accommodation which was at one of the national hotel chains. I checked in.

Apparently the police wanted me to give a brief victim impact statement at the bail hearings because the District Attorney's office had decided to request incarceration with no bail because of the violent nature of the attack against me and the fact that the two accused had wasted no time in continuing their criminal career the very day they were released from custody on Friday.

Enright had convinced me that I had a civic duty to cooperate with law enforcement to keep these criminals off the streets.

I spent the remainder of Saturday in my hotel room studying maps. In fact the only time I left my room was to walk across the street to have supper at a fast food restaurant. I was back in my room well before dark.

I had learned my lesson about being out at night in Houston.

Hurricanes were forming in the Atlantic Ocean and that made the Gulf States rather iffy as destinations at this volatile time of the weather cycle.

I tentatively charted out a route whereby I would head north in Texas and cross into Louisiana east of Jasper, Texas. At that point I would head in a northerly direction but avoid the rather large city of Shreveport, Louisiana.

I would likely enter Arkansas just south of El Dorado and stay there on

Monday night assuming that the bail hearing ended before noon.

Time would tell if my harrowing experience of being carjacked here in Houston would dampen my enthusiasm to see new territory.

A part of me was hankering to find a very small town somewhere and begin a new life.

Oddly enough I had missed my fifty-fifth birthday on the 12th of September because I had been in la-la land on that hospital cot.

Presumably I had now just entered old age. Generally speaking middle-age was considered to have ended when a guy reached age fifty-five.

Billy Swanson was now officially an old man.

CHAPTER 26 (Scary Threat)

On Sunday morning I happened to look out my hotel room window and observed a huge Hispanic man who seemed to be inordinately interested in my new car.

I took a couple of photos of the fellow with my smartphone.

I watched as he peered into the tinted windows and then walked to his own vehicle and climbed inside.

His Texas licence plate was visible from my window so I took a photo of the plate and vehicle.

As a probably unnecessary precaution, I emailed Detective Enright with the licence plate number and a brief description of the man and his SUV including the pictures I had taken and indicated that the fellow had been most curious about my new Nissan Kicks.

The man entered the hotel office and then drove off in his vehicle a few minutes later.

I didn't feel like taking my car anywhere today so I walked across the street and had a late breakfast at the fast food joint.

Just as I returned to the hotel property, an SUV pulled up beside me and the same chap I had seen earlier pointed a handgun at me and told me to get in his vehicle.

I had no choice but to obey.

"Put this bag over your head. I'm not going to hurt you but I don't want you to know where I'm taking you."

I pulled the dark cloth bag over my head and closed the drawstring.

Despite the terrifying situation, I wasn't the least bit scared. Perhaps my earlier near-death experience had convinced me that some things were totally out of our control.

Or possibly my brain had registered the sad fact that I had entered the slippery slope of old age and that the future wouldn't be rosy as a widowed and lonely old geezer.

In any event I attempted to make conversation with the driver but he told me to shut up although he did disclose that I was going to meet someone who wanted to speak with me.

After roughly thirty minutes of driving, the SUV stopped and I was led out of the vehicle with my head covering still in place.

We entered a doorway which was abruptly closed and I was rather roughly pushed onto a chair.

"Good afternoon, Mr. Swanson. I'm so sorry to have abducted you but I have a request. Please don't disappoint me by refusing what I ask. I assure you that your life is genuinely in danger both right now and again on Monday if you fail to comply with my wishes."

"I'm listening."

"At the bail hearing you'll be attending on Monday morning, I need you to recant your positive identification of the two accused gentlemen as well as state that in fact you only spent a few days in the hospital and that you are perfectly fine now."

"Actually I hadn't wanted to attend the hearing. Houston has been most unkind to me and I had intended to leave Texas yesterday after I checked out of my hotel, but Detective Enright phoned to update me on the latest shenanigans of your two associates. Enright persuaded me that it was my civic duty to remain in Houston and attend the hearing. That's what I fully intend to do."

"Can I rely on you to also accommodate my wishes?"

"Not a chance."

The speaker burst out laughing.

"I can't believe what I'm hearing. Did it not register in your legal brain that your life is in imminent danger?"

"I heard you loud and clear but your powers of persuasion are not as potent as you believe. What part of 'no way' did you not comprehend?"

"You're signing your own death warrant by defying me?"

"Maybe I'm in the process of creating a new manner of taking my own life, somewhat similar to suicide by cop. I think it should be termed suicide by criminal low-life. I'm going to be famous."

"I must admit that I wasn't expecting any level of defiance from you let alone being the subject of outright insults. Before my colleague strangles the life out of you, would you indulge me with a more detailed explanation for your surprising attitude?"

"I reached the official start of old age while I was in a coma at the hospital. I'm a widower with no kids and in fact no living relatives. I was turfed out of my government legal career by two supercilious young women less than a month ago. Even though my financial situation is rather stellar, I have no friends or purpose in life. Death no longer terrifies me. In fact everyone thought I was already dead when they found me after the carjacking."

"I don't understand what you mean."

"I'd spent more than a full day with a sheet over my entire body in the hospital morgue. A coroner was just about to cut me open in order to determine the cause of my death when he became puzzled by the lack of rigor mortis. That's when he realized to his horror that I was still alive."

"Surely telling a little fib at the bail hearing would be far preferable to dying right here, right now."

"As a matter of fact it wouldn't be the better choice. Despite being an attorney, I always maintained my ethics. I have no intention of tossing them away now. By the way, killing me will likely suck you and your large colleague into your own vortex of horror."

"Now you've got my undivided attention."

"You're operating under the mistaken belief that my presence here cannot possibly be established. In fact it will only require a minimum of police ingenuity to link Bigfoot here with my disappearance, and of course that trail will lead right to this very building unless you're far more intelligent than you sound."

"Why should I believe a legal shyster?"

"My smartphone is in the left pocket of my pants. May I ask you a question?"

"Fire away."

"Is Bigfoot's vehicle licence plate valid or a fake?"

"It's a valid Texas licence."

"In that case you are greatly underestimating your peril in harming me. Please pull out my smartphone. I'll provide you with the password to access the data. Then you can read my latest email message and make a more informed decision about my future."

I felt someone's hand go into my pocket and extract my smartphone.

"The password is BILLYTHELOSER all in large caps."

"I'm in. Now what do you want me to look at?"

"Go to the emails folder and read the message and attachments I sent to Detective Enright when I happened to notice Bigfoot lurking around my vehicle in my hotel parking lot."

"That was quite astute of you. Perhaps you wasted your career by settling for a comfy government job."

"I may have been extremely naïve when I failed to recognize and prevent the carjacking, but I'm quickly getting wiser now that I've attained old age."

"You've convinced me, Billy Swanson. My associate will drive you back to your hotel without harming you. Despite the fact that I failed to persuade you to recant your identification, I'm nevertheless pleased that we had this conversation. Believe it or not, my faith in the legal profession has been partially restored."

"Don't get carried away. Most attorneys are despicable scoundrels."

"I can't argue with you on that score. Goodbye Billy. I wish you well in your future."

My phone was placed back in my pocket and Bigfoot escorted me back to his vehicle and drove me to the hotel.

I wasn't entirely certain that I was no longer in danger until the covering was removed from my head and I realized that I was back in my hotel parking lot.

I had the good sense to keep my mouth shut during the entire drive. Sometimes silence is the wise course of inaction.

CHAPTER 27 (Rough Justice)

Once safely in my hotel room, I mulled over whether to inform Detective Enright of my most recent adventure.

In the end I decided not to further antagonize the well-spoken man who had spared my life this evening.

It was dangerous enough that I was going to defy his request and attend the bail hearing of the two carjackers where I intended to do my utmost to help persuade the judge not to let them back out on the street.

Surprisingly that evening I fell asleep moments after my head hit the pillow.

Apparently extreme danger was an effective sedative. Who would have guessed?

On Monday morning I rose early and whipped across the street for a greasy fast food breakfast.

A bit later I checked out of the hotel and drove to the police station where Detective Enright had just arrived to begin his shift. He said that he would accompany me to the bail hearing.

Enright thanked me for being cooperative and on time. He drove me to the courthouse where he inquired where the bail hearings would take place.

We found the correct courtroom where we took a seat and Enright pulled out his smartphone and began checking his emails.

After a few moments he spoke.

"I see that you sent me an email yesterday. What was that all about?"

"I got paranoid that someone was inordinately interested in my vehicle in the hotel parking lot so I sent you some photos just in case I went missing."

Enright opened my email.

"The fact that you're here this morning seems to prove that you weren't in any danger."

I didn't respond. Nothing would be gained by blurting out my kidnapping ordeal.

About a dozen rough-looking men were escorted into the courtroom and seated in the first two rows. My heart sank. With so many bail hearings to deal with, I might not be able to escape from Houston as early as I had hoped.

Neither Estevan nor Montoya were in this group of criminals. Their absence made me speculate whether another large batch of low-lifes would be escorted in once these guys were disposed of.

Enright stood up and spoke with one of the guards.

He returned to the bench where I was sitting.

"There must have been some screw-up. These are the only accused facing a bail hearing in this court today. We may as well leave. I'll try to find out what's going on."

I groaned.

It took three separate calls but finally Enright got his answer.

"Jorge Estevan and Carlos Montoya were both murdered in the jail where they were being held in custody pending the outcome of their bail hearings."

I gasped.

The fellow who had threatened me last night had doled out his own brand of rough justice once he concluded that it would be too risky to have Bigfoot murder me.

"I assume that I'm now free to leave Texas."

"That's correct. Your attendance won't be required since both of your attackers have been permanently disposed of."

"Can my Gucci wallet and wedding ring be returned to me now?"

"Let's go to the property room when we get back to the station. I'll see what I can do."

That procedure went smoothly and within thirty minutes my wedding ring was back on my finger and the wallet

Debbie had given me as a birthday present years ago was in my pocket where it belonged.

Enright again thanked me for my cooperation and wished me well. I was tempted to describe the kidnapping last night so that the cops would have at least some clue to the murders but decided not to open up that can of worms. Doing so might complicate my exit from Texas. Not only that, but there would be no evidentiary link between Bigfoot and the extermination of Estevan and Montoya in the jail.

I hopped in my Nissan pleased that I was finally saying a permanent goodbye to Houston.

CHAPTER 28 (Courtesy Call)

The quickest way to leave Houston was on Interstate 59 north which I found with no difficulty.

When I reached Livingston about an hour later, I exited the freeway at small Highway 63 and followed that route across the Sabine River into Louisiana where it became Highway 8.

I stayed on various small highways making sure to avoid the cities of Shreveport, Alexandria and Monroe.

When I entered Arkansas on small Highway 79, exhaustion overtook me and I found a hotel room in the small town of Magnolia.

I ate supper at a fast food franchise right beside the hotel and then returned to my room where I cracked open a cold can of beer which I had put on ice in a plastic wastebasket.

This was the first alcoholic drink I'd had since being released from the hospital and it tasted delicious.

I was on my third can of beer when my smartphone buzzed just before nine o'clock.

"Good evening, Billy. Did the bail hearing proceed well this morning?"

"Everything worked out for the best. The two pieces of career criminal scum who had attacked me failed to show up for their hearing. Those gentlemen both slipped in the shower at the jail and succumbed to their injuries. Lady Justice can be a cruel bitch at times."

The caller chuckled.

"Are you still in Houston?"

"I escaped from Texas shortly after I received the good news. The police even returned my Gucci wallet and wedding ring before we said our goodbyes. At this moment I'm in a hotel in a small town in Arkansas where I'm savoring my third can of cold beer."

"Please don't lie to me. Did you mention last night's meeting to the authorities?"

"I decided that no good would come of blurting out the details of my little side-trip to meet you. No evidence could ever link you or your assistant to the jail incidents and disclosing the kidnapping might complicate my own situation in that the police might insist that I remain in Houston while they investigated my allegations."

"That was a wise decision but doesn't it somewhat tarnish your concept of legal ethics?"

"That's a possibility but as far as I'm concerned, the timely demise of the two deceased gentlemen will turn out to be of great benefit to society. They've carjacked and beaten the pulp out of their last innocent victim, and for that I and the good folks of Houston thank you."

"You are entirely welcome, Billy. From my perspective, being forced to adopt a Plan B after our little discussion ended in a stalemate has turned out to be a win-win situation. My organization no longer has anything serious to fear from the loose lips of the two deceased chaps, and your freedom to move about the country has been fully restored."

"Although your brand of rough justice might be considered harsh by some, in my view the two low-lifes got precisely what they deserved."

"I don't disagree, Billy. Have a nice life."

"Thank you also for this courtesy call. It was very informative. I certainly won't forget our brief association."

I heard a chuckle and then the line went dead.

CHAPTER 29 (Vacation or Home Search)

I sucked back a fourth beer as a somewhat vindictive memorial service to the dead carjackers.

They got what they richly deserved.

My dreams were troubled but too vague to remember much about them.

On Tuesday morning I got an early start, intending to skip breakfast and eat lunch somewhere along my route today.

Although I had planned on driving north today into Missouri, at the last minute I decided to head east instead and took Highway 82 all the way across the Mississippi River into Greenville, Mississippi where I stopped for gas and lunch.

Today I was really enjoying the driving.

In fact the freedom was so intoxicating that I continued heading east on the same highway until I reached the state of Alabama. I never thought that I'd get to see any of these southern states.

Since it was getting to be late in the afternoon, I checked my map and drove north to the tiny town of Fayette where I found a private motel for the night.

I ate supper at a diner right across the street from the motel and then retired to my room to plot out the next phase of my trip.

Practically everyone I spoke to in the gas bars and restaurants had pronounced southern drawls and it dawned on me that I really wouldn't fit in if I decided to reside in the Deep South.

That prompted me to give more consideration to my future.

The more I thought about it, the more convinced I was that returning to South Dakota provided the best chance of contentment.

For one thing, I could work as an attorney if I felt like it, an option which wasn't available anywhere else. Age fifty-five struck me as too early to stop working altogether. I had intended to remain with the South Dakota government until I hit sixty-five.

There was no way I wanted to be idle for the next ten years and then for the long but indefinite period from then until I died or developed dementia.

There were several new states I might be able to travel through depending on which route I selected.

Perusing maps kept me occupied until I decided to hit the sack at ten o'clock.

On Wednesday morning I ate an early breakfast in the diner across the street and started driving north at eight o'clock.

Despite travelling on small highways, I stopped for gas at Florence and shortly thereafter made it into Tennessee just after ten o'clock.

I stayed on Highway 13 all the way through the state and reached Kentucky at one o'clock.

My choices now were to head west or continue driving north. I decided on the latter and expected to find a hotel in Indiana in a few hours.

I found a small Highway 41 which ran north parallel with the Pennyrile Parkway which was a four-lane freeway.

It took me about two and a half hours to make it into Evansville, Indiana.

After topping up my gas tank, I took a quick look at my maps.

If I didn't mind taking a bit of a western detour, then I could actually make it to Michigan. I thought about that for a couple of minutes but decided that it wasn't worth the trouble.

For one thing, my two options at that point would be impractical. I could continue north to the Upper Peninsula and then veer west, but that would entail quite a bit of additional mileage.

The second unsavory choice was to see a tiny bit of extreme southern Michigan and then head west, but that would take me through the Chicago metropolitan area which I had learned on the nightly news was probably the most dangerous city in America.

I'd already had more than my fill of huge cities and the danger which was rampant in them.

My decision wisely made, I found some small highways and half an hour later I was crossing the Wabash River into Illinois.

I continued driving for another hour and found a motel at the small city of Mt. Vernon.

It had been an enjoyable day. The weather was lovely and I was quite satisfied with my progress in making it back to South Dakota.

CHAPTER 30 (Unwanted Detour)

I must have been more exhausted than I realized because when I finally woke up on Thursday morning, it was after eleven o'clock.

I showered, dressed and then checked out of the motel.

On my way out of Mt. Vernon I spotted a pleasant looking restaurant and decided to have lunch there. I was in no hurry today.

My intention was to head west for about twenty miles and then turn north in order to avoid the large and dangerous city of St. Louis, Missouri.

From my maps I had discovered that there weren't very many spots to cross the Mississippi River. My intention was to take small highways north well past St. Louis and then veer west and enter the state of Missouri either at Highway 54 or further north at Quincy.

Lunch was delicious and it was almost one o'clock by the time I had finished eating and used the washroom.

Since I was getting a bit low on money, I stopped at a branch of my bank and withdrew $2,000 in cash.

I finally began driving west on Highway 15.

Within ten miles I saw a Black girl walking on the shoulder of the road with a child who looked to be no more than six or seven years old.

There was virtually no traffic on this small highway.

As I got nearer to the two pedestrians, the girl waved me down.

Even though I was leery of stopping for a stranger, there were no ditches or bushes near the road from which some male accomplice could rush out and attack me.

I pulled onto the shoulder of the road and rolled down my passenger door window.

"Can I help you, young lady?"

"My kid and I are flat broke. We've been walking for the past hour but nobody seems to want to give us a ride. We're both beat. Can we trouble you to drive us in to St. Louis?"

"I had intended to avoid the city but that decision isn't set in stone. Hop in and I'll take you there."

"Thanks so much, mister. This has been a terrible day for Billy and me."

"Is that your son's name."

"Yeah."

"My name's also Billy. How did your day get all fouled up?"

"Billy and me are in a real mess. My great aunt lives in Mt. Vernon and we caught a ride there first thing this morning with one of the tenants in the old house we live at. It turns out that my great aunt wasn't so thrilled to see me and she refused to help us out. Going there was a complete waste of time."

"Why didn't you phone her first?"

"I don't own a phone and neither does Aunt Violet. Going there in person was the only choice. I took Billy with me because I wasn't sure if I'd be back home by the time his school was out."

"What sort of mess are you in?"

"I missed our weekly rent payment last Thursday and the landlord threatened to throw us out in the street if I didn't make that payment plus tomorrow's payment."

"How much is your weekly rent?"

"It's a hundred and forty bucks a week. Aunt Violet was our last hope. Billy and me will have to go to some filthy homeless shelter if our landlord kicks us out tomorrow."

"That is a real problem. Do you not have a job?"

"I work in a diner but my boss is having a tough time making ends meet. My hours got cut and Billy had a bad toothache a couple of weeks ago. The dentist refused to see Billy unless I paid cash up front and we ain't on welfare. That meant that I didn't have any money left to pay our rent."

"I take it that you don't have a credit card you can use to bail yourself out of the jam you're in."

"Credit cards are poison for folks like me who are struggling to make ends meet. It's the same thing with the payday loan places. I got in hock with one of them a couple of years ago and it was almost impossible to finally pay them off and get them off my back. Their late charges are awful."

The girl said that her name was Jasmine and that she was twenty-four. Billy's father took off for parts unknown long before Billy was born and Jasmine's parents were dead. She had no brothers or sisters.

Jasmine asked me why I was on this tiny highway and I told her about retiring recently and treating myself to a driving trip to see parts of America I'd never seen before.

"How come your wife didn't come with you? That's a wedding ring on your left hand."

"My wife passed away four years ago. I miss her terribly and feel that by wearing the ring she gave me when we got married, a small piece of her is still with me."

"That's a real nice thing to say, mister."

I didn't mention my carjacking and kidnapping adventures. In all likelihood Jasmine wouldn't have believed me anyway.

We crossed the Mississippi River into St. Louis, Missouri.

The traffic was tolerable at this time of day.

Jasmine directed me to her neighborhood which was very poor and appeared to be exceedingly dangerous.

I wasn't comfortable being here. My new car sported a Texas licence plate which again marked me as a lost tourist.

This was definitely an unwanted detour.

CHAPTER 31 (Generous Attorney)

When we pulled into the driveway at the dilapidated old house where Jasmine rented a tiny apartment, I was quite appalled.

A couple of derelict cars were up on blocks in the parking area and several of the houses on the street were either for sale under foreclosure or boarded up.

This part of St. Louis was the poster child for abject poverty and societal failure.

Just seeing the squalor here accentuated the inability of our governments to manage society.

America was sending tens of billions of dollars to finance a questionable war in Ukraine but sat idly by while St. Louis degenerated into this third-world atrocity.

Residing in the wealthy but remote small city of Pierre, South Dakota and never traveling out of the state until this past month had blinded me to the putrid state of my beloved country.

Even though I had watched some segments on Fox News about the homeless problem in many large cities, it was impossible to comprehend the depressing reality from a television broadcast.

The overall problem was far above my pay grade to resolve but as Jasmine and young Billy opened their doors to exit my vehicle, it struck me that I could at least eradicate their immediate catastrophe.

I removed my seat belt and stepped out of the car.

In addition to stretching my legs for a moment, I had another goal.

It was fortunate that I'd dropped in to the bank in Mt. Vernon.

As Jasmine stood wide-eyed with her jaw gaping open, I counted out $750.

"This is my gift to you and Billy. It will allow you to pay your rent and hopefully provide you with the time to get back on your feet financially. I wish you and Billy all the best in life."

I handed the cash to Jasmine who threw her arms around me and thanked me. There were tears in her eyes and I felt good knowing that at least I was able to solve one tiny problem for a fellow human being at least for a brief time.

I got back in my vehicle and started it up. I rolled my window down several inches because Jasmine wanted to say something.

"I really believe that God sent you to us, mister. I was sick with worry that Billy and me were going to be out on the street tomorrow. You're a lifesaver."

"It was a remarkable coincidence that our paths crossed, Jasmine. I so hope that everything will work out wonderfully for you and Billy."

I asked Jasmine how to get to get to a highway from this neighborhood.

She gave me some directions to find Interstate 70 and we bade each other goodbye.

As I drove away, I couldn't help but lament the incredible poverty all around me.

It was overwhelmingly sad and I cursed the politicians who had allowed this travesty to develop.

CHAPTER 32 (History Repeats)

Jasmine's directions proved to be a bit confusing and I passed street after street of squalor.

Even though it was the middle of the afternoon on a bright and sunny day, I was too timid to stop anywhere to ask for better directions. I had learned my lesson from Houston.

Presumably I would reach some highway at some point all on my own.

I seemed to be the only operational vehicle on these particular streets although there were an untold number of beat-up and probably derelict cars either in driveways or parked on the street.

There was a stop sign at the next intersection and I hoped that meant that I'd be able to turn onto a more heavily travelled street and eventually find some highway sign which I could follow.

I came to a full and complete stop at the stop sign. The last thing I needed now was to get a ticket for some silly traffic infraction.

I sensed some commotion to my left and turned my head to see what was going on.

A Black man in a hoodie was just two feet away from me waving a gun around.

"Turn your fucking engine off," he screamed through the partially open driver's window.

I was petrified but put the gearshift in park and then reached down and pressed the engine off button.

"Unlock the door and get the fuck out of the car."

My mind was racing.

This guy seemed to be drugged out of his mind or just plain crazy.

If I did as he demanded, he would likely shoot me before robbing me and driving off in my Nissan.

It was a terrible choice to be forced to make.

Should I die inside my car or be robbed and shot on the dirty pavement?

The old adage that no good deed goes unpunished sprang into my mind.

Giving Jasmine and Billy a ride home and then handing her enough cash to bail her out of her jam was now going to get me murdered in a strange city.

God may have been looking after Jasmine but He must have forgotten all about me.

My mind darted back to my current predicament.

The crazy guy was still yelling at me to get out of the car or he'd shoot me where I sat.

I made my decision.

Dying inside my car was preferable to succumbing to this scumbag's demands.

I reached down in order to start the engine back up.

That infuriated my assailant who stuck his gun in the open window and pressed it against my temple.

"I warned you, old man. Now you're going to die."

I no longer felt the gun against my head so I glanced toward the guy threatening me.

He had moved back a foot or two and was in the process of pulling the trigger of his gun which was aimed directly at my head.

Reflexively I jerked forward and heard an incredibly loud bang.

Suddenly the back of my neck stung and I realized that my life was over.

CHAPTER 33 (Timely Intervention)

I heard shouting but was too dazed to make out the words.

Then shots rang out which thoroughly confused me because I couldn't feel any bullets striking me anywhere.

I turned my head toward the attacker which gave me a front row seat to the action.

He was shooting at someone else.

Suddenly I watched in horror as his face changed shape while blood and brain matter splattered against my car window. Some of the fleshy debris sprayed through the open portion of the window and struck my own face.

Nothing made any sense.

I was so shocked that I couldn't comprehend what was taking place.

I just sat in my car like a zombie.

More voices bombarded me but I couldn't distinguish the words.

Finally it registered in my brain what was happening.

Someone was asking me to unlock my car door but I just sat there like a ventriloquist's dummy.

I sensed an arm reaching in through the window and watched in disbelief as it felt around for the locking mechanism and unlocked the door.

As the door was pulled open, I realized that a police officer was standing beside the car.

"Have you been shot, sir?"

"I don't know. The back of my neck is stinging. I saw the face of that carjacker disintegrate right before my eyes."

"We had to use deadly force to save your life and our own. We saw him shoot at you from point blank range. We assumed that he had killed you but the shooter immediately began shooting at us. We returned fire. Thank God that you're still alive. An ambulance has been summoned. Are you strong enough to step out of your vehicle?"

"I'll give it a try, officer."

I released my seatbelt and gingerly climbed out of my Nissan.

The body of the carjacker was lying beside my car and I got another look at the pulpy remains of his face. It was the stuff of nightmares.

The cop examined my neck area and informed me that the shooter's bullet must have grazed the back of my neck which was bleeding slightly.

He bent down to examine the interior of my Nissan.

"I can see where the bullet has embedded itself in your passenger door. I don't know how the shooter missed killing you at such close range."

"I saw him squeezing the trigger and instinctively lurched forward. He was apoplectic because I refused to unlock my door and get out of the car. On the spur of the moment I had decided that I'd rather die inside my vehicle than outside on the road."

An ambulance arrived.

The paramedics very quickly determined that the carjacker was dead.

One of them examined me and put some antiseptic lotion on the back of my neck and then covered the small wound with a bandage.

My somewhat bizarre sense of humor returned.

"Could I trouble you to get me a towel so that I can wipe the carjacker's brain matter off my face?"

The cops and the paramedics burst out laughing.

Sometimes humor was the best antidote for horror.

CHAPTER 34 (Explanation)

I was still in shock but advised the police and paramedics that I didn't want to be taken to the hospital although I admitted that I was too shaken up to drive my car.

Since my golf shirt was stained from the flying brain matter, the cops let me remove the shirt which I gave them to keep as evidence. I sure didn't want it back. I put a clean shirt on from a sports bag in my trunk.

It was a wonder that I hadn't messed my pants but there was no sign of any involuntary urinary or bowel discharge on my pants.

The police called for a tow truck to take my Nissan to a police garage where the bullet could be extracted from the passenger door and the vehicle properly examined.

I was driven in the police car to the station so that I could provide a proper statement regarding what had just occurred.

The cop who drove me said that because it was a Black man who had been shot, it was crucial that the shooting be shown to have been justified before the media distorted the facts in order to push their narrative that the St.

Louis police were racist. In this case both police officers at the scene were also Black but ideologues often ignored facts in order to further their goals.

At the station I was allowed to wash up in a lavatory before the interview. There were still bits of fleshy residue on me which the dry towel had not been successful in wiping away.

I was totally grossed out.

At the interview, which was being recorded, I was asked to explain the sequence of events.

"I had gotten a bit lost. I had obtained directions to get to Interstate 70 but either those directions were faulty or I misheard them, because I wound up driving around rather haphazardly."

"What happened at that intersection?"

I related the incident from the moment I stopped for the stop sign until the police officer reached in the partially open window and opened the driver's door.

They were particularly interested in my confirmation that the carjacker had actually shot at me.

They had taken photos of my neck wound as well as the bullet hole in the passenger door.

"Your vehicle has a Texas licence plate and your vehicle has a Barrett,

Texas dealer's advertisement on the plate holder. Do you live in Texas?"

"No. I used to reside in Pierre, South Dakota but I was forced to retire at the end of August. I vacated my apartment and I've been on a driving trip ever since August 31st? At the moment I have no home address."

"Why did you purchase a vehicle in Texas? Didn't you already own a car in South Dakota?"

"I did have an almost identical Nissan Kicks but it was stolen in Houston and my insurance company made arrangements for me to purchase a replacement vehicle in Barrett, Texas because that dealership happened to have a 2023 Nissan Kicks in stock."

"How did your previous car get stolen in Houston?"

"I was carjacked and left for dead behind a gas station after getting lost in Houston after dark. I was in a coma for several days and then suffered from amnesia for a short while after I woke up. I thought lightning never struck in the same place twice. Today was the second time this month that I've been the victim of a carjacking."

The police never pursued their original question regarding why I was in a derelict neighborhood in St. Louis in the first place.

I decided not to enlighten them. The last thing I wanted was to be publicized as some sort of tragic hero who faced intense danger all because he had helped out someone in dire need of a ride and a financial bailout.

One thing puzzled me so I asked.

"I thought police response time was a real problem these days. How did you guys show up at the carjacking so promptly?"

"Someone, probably the same guy, tried to carjack a vehicle in that general area about twenty minutes earlier. We were cruising around looking for him when we spotted your vehicle and the carjacker pointing his gun at you. The rest is history."

I was driven to a hotel near the police station where I paid for a room for the night.

The police indicated that they would thoroughly clean my vehicle after they had removed the bullet. They fully expected that the Nissan could be released to me tomorrow.

I was adamant that I didn't want to speak with any media about the incident and the cops respected my wishes although they replied that they would definitely contact the media in order to get the truth out there immediately.

Once inside my hotel room, I showered more thoroughly than I ever had before.

For supper I ordered room service. All I wanted was to stay safe and secure inside my own room.

CHAPTER 35 (Fleeting Fame)

Everything went relatively smoothly on Friday.

I ate breakfast in the hotel dining-room and felt that the ordeal was pretty much behind me.

I hadn't suffered from any nightmares or delayed mental trauma.

Billy Swanson had yet again simply been in the wrong place at the wrong time.

Someone from the police department called me on my smartphone shortly after breakfast.

Their investigation of my vehicle had been completed and they had both the interior and exterior properly cleaned. If convenient, someone could come to my hotel and drive me to the garage where I could pick up my car and continue on my driving journey.

That suited me perfectly and I agreed to check out of the hotel and wait at the front entrance to be picked up.

When a female police officer arrived about thirty minutes later, she handed me this morning's edition of the main local newspaper.

"The story about your ordeal is on Page 7. The department wanted to get the story out as quickly as possible in order to prevent any civic unrest."

"I'll read the piece after I've left St. Louis. No offence, but I can't wait to get back on the open road. Believe me, I'm going to avoid travelling through any more big cities. They're far too dangerous for an aging attorney like me to handle."

The officer chuckled.

My car looked great although the hole in the passenger door where the carjacker's bullet had been extracted was still a stark reminder of my latest near-death experience.

I was given specific and easy to follow directions by the police officer to the nearest on-ramp of Interstate 70.

In fact she had me follow her squad car to the on-ramp. I waved my thank-you and was soon heading west out of St. Louis.

At the suburb of St. Peters, I got off the interstate and took small Highway 79 for just over an hour at which point I veered east on Highway 36.

Just before four o'clock I reached St. Joseph and then crossed the Missouri River into the northeast corner of Kansas.

An hour later I entered Nebraska and got a hotel room at the small city of Falls City.

I was still spooked by yesterday's carjacking, so I had purchased a submarine sandwich when I stopped for gas in Falls City before finding accommodation.

I ate the sub with a cold Pepsi in my hotel room.

Afterwards I looked at maps and decided that the city of Huron, South Dakota should make a satisfactory place in which to settle down for the next phase of my life. Huron was virtually the same population as Pierre and had a reputation of being extremely safe albeit somewhat boring. That description suited my current mind-set perfectly.

I remembered that the police officer had given me a copy of today's St. Louis newspaper. I went down to the parking lot and retrieved the publication from my Nissan.

Back in the room, I opened the paper to page 7 and spotted the headline.

ST. LOUIS POLICE SAVE TOURIST FROM CERTAIN DEATH

William Swanson owes his life to the quick action of the St. Louis Police Department.

While searching for a reported carjacker, police were roaming the Delmar Blvd. neighborhood and happened upon a violent carjacking in progress.

The attacker had a gun pointed inside a vehicle at a motorist who was stopped at an intersection.

The motorist was understandably reluctant to exit his car and that enraged the criminal who shot the driver.

Police ordered the perpetrator to drop his firearm but instead he began firing at the law enforcement officers.

They returned fire and killed the carjacker, a career criminal named DeVon Carter with a lengthy record going back to 2009. In fact Carter had been released without bail two weeks earlier following his arrest for an earlier carjacking and various drug-related charges.

Police expected to find the driver dead inside his car but Mr. Swanson had Lady Luck on his side. He had watched in horror as the carjacker began to squeeze the trigger with the gun aimed directly at Swanson's face.

Swanson lurched forward just as the bullet flew past him grazing his neck and then embedding itself in the passenger door.

Although Swanson was in shock, his wound was thankfully superficial and *paramedics at the crime scene were able to stop the bleeding.*

Bits of flesh and other bodily matter from DeVon Carter had splattered through the open window onto Swanson's face and clothing.

Swanson explained that he was a tourist from Texas who had inadvertently gotten lost in that section of St. Louis and was attempting to find his way to Interstate 70.

As a gesture of goodwill, police cleaned Swanson's vehicle thoroughly after extracting the bullet from the passenger side door.

Our reporters were unable to contact Swanson who had informed police that he wished to remain as anonymous as possible. We did learn that William Swanson is a retired Texas attorney and that he was a victim earlier this month of another carjacking in Houston.

This reporter can only conclude that some lawyers are like cats and have nine lives.

I sat back and reflected on the newspaper piece. It was surprisingly accurate and luckily didn't contain sufficient information from which I could be identified.

The Houston carjacking never even made it into the newspapers because of the time gap between the crime and my reawakening.

This St. Louis story was to be my only claim to fleeting media fame.

CHAPTER 36 (New Home)

On Saturday morning I woke quite refreshed after a solid and uninterrupted sleep.

Today was the first day of October and I was hoping that this would turn out to be a much less chaotic month than September had tormented me with.

I started driving at eight o'clock, heading west first before turning north on Highway 81.

At half past two I entered South Dakota at Yankton. It was still about a hundred and thirty miles to Huron but I was anxious to make it there today.

Finally shortly after five o'clock I arrived at the small city I had decided to call my new home.

The population of Huron was roughly 14,000 and it was the county seat of Beadle County.

I got a hotel room first and then treated myself to supper and a beer at a sit-down restaurant near my hotel.

After supper I read a complimentary copy of the local community newspaper which had a real estate section.

One listing immediately caught my eye.

A one-bedroom ground floor condominium was for sale in town for the very reasonable price of $64,900. This was a two-storey building with a communal garage for indoor parking.

The listing realtor showed her email address in the advertisement. I sent a message from my smartphone that I had just arrived in Huron and would be interested in viewing the condominium tomorrow or Monday.

The realtor called me within ten minutes and introduced herself as Wanda Allen.

She answered any questions I had about her listing and pried out of me that I was a retired attorney from Pierre who would be paying cash and preferred a very quick closing. The unit was vacant and I mentioned that I would be willing to rent the condo immediately and continue until the closing date if that suited the owner.

We made an appointment for one o'clock tomorrow at which time I would meet her at the condominium complex.

My mood was quite upbeat as I lay in bed before falling asleep. I had survived two brutal carjacking attempts in two separate cities and lived to tell about it.

If I subtracted those violent incidents from the equation, then my retirement driving journey had actually been quite wonderful.

The highlight was easily the Riverwalk in San Antonio but a distant second was the overall scenery as I made my way around a large section of America.

In my mind I tried to count the number of states I'd visited. Including South Dakota, my mental tally reached twenty. Not too many folks could brag that they had seen parts of twenty American states.

On Sunday morning I ate a late breakfast in the hotel restaurant and booked my room for tonight.

Before I knew it, it was time to head to the condominium complex to meet the realtor.

CHAPTER 37 (A Perfect Fit)

The condominium complex was a two-storey low rise building comprising about eighteen units. I thought it was quite attractive from the front.

Wanda arrived a few minutes after me. I had wanted to walk around the exterior of the complex as well as drive around the neighborhood first.

Before we entered the building, Wanda showed me the actual listing along with a very recent certificate from the property management firm setting out the financial and structural status of the complex.

Apparently the condominium unit had been sold in July but that deal fell through when the purchasers' financing fell through at the very last minute.

The actual unit was perfect for me. It had attractive wall-too-wall carpet in the living-room and bedroom. The kitchen was a bit dated but that didn't bother me. The complex had been built in 1975.

The unit was 700 square feet and I was quite smitten with it the moment I stepped inside.

Wanda showed me the communal garage area. My unit came with one indoor parking space. There were no laundry facilities in the individual units but there were several washers and dryers in the common area in the basement.

The unit was completely empty except for the fridge, stove, dishwasher and window coverings.

Since Wanda was the listing agent, I realized that technically she was representing the vendor and her job was to obtain the best possible terms for the lady who owned the unit. That woman had moved to Sioux Falls in July.

I indicated that I was quite interested and agreed to follow Wanda back to her realty office where she would prepare a formal offer to purchase the unit.

Her realty business turned out to be a tiny office on a side street which Wanda mentioned she ran all by herself. She had no other sales agents or secretarial staff.

I agreed to accept the unit in "as is" condition since I was already satisfied with the recent status certificate.

Although Wanda tried to persuade me to offer full price, I made my offer for $60,000 with a closing date of Friday, October 7th and the proviso that I could take possession tomorrow if I paid the purchase funds in trust to the seller's attorney.

Wanda phoned the owner who agreed to accept my offer without any changes whatsoever.

I signed the offer and Wanda emailed it to the seller who accepted.

Wanda dealt with the seller's attorney all the time so Wanda called that lawyer at home and the attorney agreed to represent both the seller and me.

I transferred the deposit by telephone banking into the realty company's trust account while I was in the office and was even able to transfer the purchase funds into the lawyer's trust account.

Tomorrow morning I would attend at the attorney's office to meet the woman and she would confirm that she had received the funds.

At that point I would be given a key.

I thanked Wanda for seeing me on a Sunday afternoon and being so accommodating.

From the realty office I drove directly to a large used furniture outlet where I purchased a lovely bedroom set as well as some living-room furniture, a computer desk and a small kitchen table with two chairs.

The items would be delivered tomorrow afternoon.

I was quite thrilled with all my purchases and was greatly looking forward to being settled in my new home.

By the time I'd completed my shopping, it was time for supper. I celebrated at a sit-down restaurant and gorged myself on a huge meal.

Monday went very smoothly. I checked out of my hotel and then found a diner where I had a full breakfast.

There were no glitches regarding the purchase funds and I received my keys at ten o'clock in the morning.

While I waited for the furniture to be delivered, I made a list of household items I would need to purchase.

By three o'clock my condo looked like it was occupied.

I went out shopping and found virtually everything on my list.

Billy Swanson was soon to be a homeowner again and he was already ensconced in his new digs.

Huron seemed so far to have been an ideal choice for my new home.

CHAPTER 38 (Filling My Time)

For the remainder of the week I learned what I could about the businesses and retail outlets in Huron.

Even though I didn't need to supplement my retirement income, I really wasn't a volunteer type of guy. I had very little sympathy for deadbeats and accordingly had no desire to donate my time to a food bank or other form of charity now that I had so much free time available.

Debbie and I had spent considerable time assisting various local charities but really I had just tagged along in order to be with her. Debbie was the compassionate one. I was moderately hard-hearted. Once Debbie died I had stopped my charity work altogether.

Common sense prevailed and I realized that opening up my own legal office would be foolish since I had forgotten virtually everything I'd ever learned about the practical areas of the law I would be expected to handle.

I would have to find other ways of filling my time.

My condominium sale closed as scheduled on Friday, the 7th of October.

That meant that I was now glued at least for the time being to Huron, South Dakota.

Since the weather was very pleasant, I began a routine of going for long walks early in the morning and then stopping for breakfast at a diner I liked downtown.

It was important for me to develop a routine which was both healthy and enjoyable.

As far as whether I wanted to join any local clubs, I hadn't found anything by the middle of October which suited me. There was no duplicate bridge club in Huron and I just wasn't the health club type. I had no desire to lift weights or use any exercise equipment. My daily walks would keep me in shape.

The evenings tended to drag a bit.

I had purchased a television and now subscribed to a cable TV service but found that I didn't enjoy any of the movies or regular programs being offered.

I did watch Fox News on weekday evenings, especially the Tucker Carlson show.

To enhance my rather lonely existence, I also bought a desktop computer with a nice big screen. Scouring the internet on my smartphone was not very satisfying because the screen was so tiny.

Wanda Allen emailed me on Monday, the 17th of October. The seller had located two more keys to my condo as well as the warranties for the appliances. The woman had mailed those items to Wanda to pass along to me and they had just arrived in the mail.

I responded that I would drop by Wanda's realty office in the next day or so and pick up the items.

My left hand got caught in the oven door while I was closing it and although I wasn't hurt, my wedding ring came apart. It had been worn very thin at the back and this attack from the stove was just enough to split the ring at that weak point.

I put Debbie's ring in my desk drawer and would look for a jewellery repair shop during my morning walks. In a way it was a bit sad that I still wore the ring even though my darling wife had been dead for more than four years.

Perhaps now would be the right time to stop pretending that I was still married.

CHAPTER 39 (Friendly Conversation)

On Tuesday after my walk followed by breakfast in the diner, I dropped in to Wanda's real estate office in order to pick up the items she had received from the seller.

A very attractive woman was sitting on one of the three chairs in the waiting room but there was no sign of Wanda.

I smiled at the lady and said good morning.

She explained her presence.

"I just dropped in without an appointment to speak with a real estate agent. You can be served first."

"That's very kind of you. I'm just here to pick up some spare keys for a condominium I just purchased here in town. I won't hold you up at all."

"Have you resided in Huron long?" she asked.

"No, I just moved here two weeks ago. Is this your home town?"

"I'm new to the area as well. I bought a home in town in July in order to be near my daughter and grandkids, but my son-in-law's job got transferred yet again, this time to Omaha and they moved to Nebraska last month. Suddenly I find myself stuck in a strange city where I don't know anyone. I thought I'd speak with a realtor about possibly selling my home already."

"That's a shame. Will you move to Omaha?"

"I detest big cities. Until I moved here I had lived in a very small town in the extreme southern portion of Iowa all my life. My husband Carl died three years ago and then just last year my daughter Grace and her family moved here because of her husband's job. Where did you live before you moved to Huron?"

"Although I grew up in a small town in South Dakota, I spent my college and law school years studying in Pierre and then I worked for the state government there for the next thirty years. I was forced to take early retirement at the end of August and decided that I didn't want to live in Pierre any longer."

"Why is that?"

"My wife Debbie died four years ago and we had no children. I was quite humiliated to be effectively sacked from the position I'd held for so long, so I decided that I needed a complete change of venue."

"How's that working out for you so far?"

"The jury is still out. I haven't met any friends here yet so it's a bit on the lonely side. I vacated my apartment in Pierre on August 31st and took a long driving trip to start my retirement. At that time I had no idea where I might settle down."

"What made you choose Huron?"

"I had some harrowing adventures on my driving trip and decided that South Dakota was safe unlike other parts of America. Huron was about the same size as Pierre and I thought that remaining in South Dakota would allow me to practice law if I wanted to try my hand at operating my own legal practice."

"Is that what you intend to do?"

"No, I decided that I knew absolutely nothing about the areas of law a sole practitioner would deal with. My job with the government was highly specialized and provided no practical experience whatsoever. Are you looking for a job in Huron?"

"I'm not. I ran my own bookstore in Centreville, Iowa but sold it this spring when I decided to move to Huron. What sort of excitement did you encounter on your driving trip?"

"I really don't think that you'd believe me if I told you."

"Are you implying that folks don't trust what attorneys say?"

I laughed.

"There wouldn't be enough time to relate the incidents in all their gory detail."

At that moment Wanda emerged from the inner office with a young couple.

Wanda spotted me.

"I'm sorry to keep you and your lady friend waiting, Billy. Here are the items the vendor mailed to the office for you. It's fortunate that you came by when you did. I'm just about to close the office for an hour or so while I show these folks some homes."

Wanda handed me an envelope.

The woman I'd been chatting with didn't say anything presumably because she realized that Wanda was busy at the moment.

CHAPTER 40 (Teller of Tall Tales)

The lady and I both stood up and exited the realty office.

"Since Wanda can't see you right now, would you like to join me for coffee so that I can tell you all about my disastrous retirement driving trip?"

"That would be lovely. By the way, my name is Phoebe Carlyle."

"I'm Billy Swanson. There's a diner on the next street where I eat breakfast most mornings. Let's go there and you can decide whether I'm a demented liar or the victim of some unfortunate travel nightmares."

I couldn't help but notice that Phoebe was a very attractive lady. She had medium-length blonde hair, a slender figure and a lovely face. My best guess was that she was probably in her forties.

We made small talk on the way to the restaurant where we each ordered coffee and a slice of pie. Phoebe told me a bit about her daughter and two grandchildren. I admitted that I had no living close relatives since I'd been an only child.

The diner was exceedingly quiet since it was only ten o'clock in the morning.

Before I began the description of my driving trip, I explained to Phoebe how two young women had unceremoniously terminated my employment with the state government and intended to replace me with a computer program. I admitted that my job was highly specialized and involved drafting accurate clauses for various state laws and regulations.

I also told Phoebe about how unappreciated I had felt when I was forced into early retirement and had dreaded running in to my former coworkers because of my embarrassment at having gotten the sack.

"I'd never been out of South Dakota in my entire life but I vacated my apartment and left Pierre on the last day of August. I had no intention of returning to either Pierre or South Dakota but circumstances intervened which convinced me that this is one of the safest places to live in America."

"Did you and your late wife never travel?"

"We spent all of our vacation time either in Pierre or visiting Debbie's family in the tiny town of Avon in extreme southern South Dakota. Debbie was somewhat prone to motion sickness so air travel and long bus trips were out of the question. Did you and Carl travel a lot?"

"We took a honeymoon cruise in the Caribbean but then Grace was born the following year and we put in a swimming pool and spent our holidays at home amusing our daughter. But we digress. Tell me about your driving trip."

I gave Phoebe a fairly detailed itinerary of the first portion of the trip which culminated in my fantastic visit to the Riverwalk in San Antonio.

Then I described the drive in the rain to Houston and getting lost there because of a detour.

"I parked at a small gas station in order to ask for directions to Interstate 10 but as I was stepping out of my car, two men attacked me. They knocked me unconscious and dragged me behind the building where they stole my car key, my wallet and my wedding ring. They left me for dead and took off in my almost brand new vehicle."

Phoebe was shocked and commented about how understandable it was that I would want to return to the safety of small town South Dakota.

"That ordeal was bad enough but things quickly got worse."

I told Phoebe about the paramedics and the hospital believing that I was dead and that the old coroner finally realized that I was still alive just before he was about to carve me up in order to determine the cause of death.

Phoebe listened with rapt attention as I proceeded to tell her about my amnesia and brief hospital stay as well as the quick settlement of the lawsuit against the paramedic company and the hospital.

I decided to omit the abduction part of the story and the murder of the two carjackers.

"Billy, that's absolutely horrible."

"That was only the first nasty incident. Believe it or not, I was the victim of a second attempted carjacking about three weeks later, this time in St. Louis."

I told Phoebe about picking up Jasmine and her young son and driving them home to St. Louis even though I had intended to avoid all big cities.

I omitted my monetary gift to Jasmine and jumped to the abject horror of having a gun pointed at my head and the subsequent excitement which left me alive and the carjacker dead.

Phoebe was beginning to look a bit uncomfortable and it suddenly struck me why.

"I can see that you're starting to disbelieve me."

Phoebe blushed.

"I assure you that I'm not a nut-job but I won't hold your skepticism against you. I realize that I look like the most boring man on the planet and that was true up until I retired. Now I've turned into some sort of danger junkie. Thank you for joining me here, Phoebe. I'd better let you get back to the realty office."

I paid the tab and Phoebe thanked me for the coffee and pie.

I bade her goodbye and walked back to my condominium.

It was both insulting and upsetting to have a stranger adopt the opinion that I was some sort of demented teller of tall tales.

CHAPTER 41 (Stunning Discovery)

Phoebe Carlyle walked back to her car.

She was embarrassed to have allowed herself to join a complete stranger for coffee, but Billy had seemed so nice at the realty office.

It was a bit off-putting to have discovered that the man lived in some strange sort of fantasy land. Surely he didn't believe that spewing out a series of lies would somehow impress Phoebe.

She cursed Carl for turning into a workaholic and dying on Phoebe when he was only fifty-two.

Now here she was stranded in a strange state with no friends or family.

The realty office was open when Phoebe arrived there so she wandered inside to speak with the agent.

That brief conversation went poorly. Apparently Phoebe's timing had been bad. The home she had purchased just a few months ago was no longer worth what she had paid for it.

She drove to her house and sat in her study examining her finances. Phoebe needed to decide whether she wanted to lose at least $40,000 if she put her home up for sale. Wanda had suggested that because the quiet winter season was fast approaching, it might make more sense to wait for the spring real estate market.

Phoebe's thoughts went back to Billy Swanson and his delusions.

She got on the internet and tried to find out something about the man.

Phoebe found a couple of mentions of William Swanson in the Pierre newspapers relating to some community functions and one of those stories contained a group photo from which Phoebe could confirm that the person identified as William Swanson did appear to be the same chap Phoebe had just shared a coffee with.

She also found the obituary for Deborah Swanson. Billy hadn't been lying about his personal life.

On a whim Phoebe searched the St. Louis newspaper website and typed in "William Swanson carjacking."

Surprisingly a brief article appeared.

Phoebe read the piece and realized that Billy had been telling the truth after all. The poor man had been accosted by a carjacker and actually shot while he sat in his own car. Fortunately the bullet had only grazed the back of Billy's neck because he had lurched forward when he saw the carjacker squeezing the trigger of the gun.

The article even confirmed that Billy had been the victim in an earlier carjacking in Houston.

The only discrepancy between the newspaper article and Billy's account of the ordeal was that the paper described Billy as a retired Texas attorney.

Phoebe felt terrible that she hadn't believed Billy and had been so obvious about her skepticism.

She had no idea where Billy lived and didn't feel comfortable calling the realty office to find out.

Billy had mentioned that he ate breakfast at the diner most mornings.

Phoebe would apologize to Billy if and when she happened to spot him when he was having his breakfast.

CHAPTER 42 (Second Chances)

On Wednesday I went for my morning walk and stopped at my usual diner for breakfast.

I had no sooner sat down when Phoebe walked in and came directly to the booth where I was sitting.

"Good morning, Billy. Would you mind terribly if I joined you for breakfast?"

"That would be my pleasure, Phoebe. I must admit that I'm surprised to see you. I got the distinct impression yesterday that you thought I was the teller of whoppers."

"I'm embarrassed to admit that I didn't believe you but when I got home my curiosity got the better of me and I looked you up on the internet. I not only confirmed that you had resided in Pierre but I also located the newspaper article describing your carjacking nightmare in St. Louis. Please accept my sincere apologies for my behavior yesterday."

"There's no need to apologize. I fully realized that my twin carjacking ordeals would be difficult for anyone to swallow. Other than the police who were at the St. Louis crime scene, you're the only person I've dared to tell about my unsolicited vacation excitement."

The waitress appeared with coffee and also took our breakfast order.

"The only part of the newspaper article that confused me was when it described you as a retired Texas attorney."

"My first Nissan was never recovered after the Houston carjacking. When I came out of my coma, my insurance company arranged to purchase for me an almost identical replacement vehicle from a dealer in Texas. That vehicle came with a set of Texas licence plates and the reporter must have assumed that I was from Texas. I never spoke with anyone from the paper. They got their information from the police."

Phoebe and I had a marvelous morning discussing in great detail each of my carjacking episodes.

In fact she was so easy to talk to that I even blurted out the follow-up story of my abduction by the car theft gang leader and the subsequent murder in jail of the two carjackers.

I repeated the joke about lawyers perhaps having nine lives just like cats.

Phoebe and I bonded over the course of the morning and she invited me for supper this evening at her home.

We spent the rest of the day together. I showed Phoebe my new condominium as well as the bullet hole in the passenger door of my Nissan.

Supper was a pure joy and by the end of the evening, I had made a fantastic new friend.

Even though Phoebe looked to be in her early forties, in fact she was only one year younger than me. Some women just age well.

Romance had entered the picture by the end of our first week glued to each other.

Within a month I had moved in with Phoebe and we were totally and utterly in love.

For the time being my condominium remained vacant. We didn't feel comfortable renting it out so we decided to keep it for now. Phoebe's family could use the condo as their own private accommodation whenever they visited Huron which was about 225 miles from Omaha.

Phoebe and I decided to do some travelling together.

We've booked a fourteen day Caribbean cruise which will depart from Miami on December 20th and return on January 3rd.

Somehow Lady Luck or perhaps even God stepped in to turn my lonely life into an ocean of love and companionship.

   This carjacked lawyer had landed on his feet and my life was absolutely glorious.

   THE END

ABOUT THE AUTHOR

Donald W. Desaulniers is a Canadian lawyer who operated his own legal practice in the picturesque small city of Belleville, Ontario from 1973 until he retired in 2009.

He still resides in Belleville with his lovely British wife, Jane and their cat Charlie. Donald is a graduate of University of Waterloo (1968) and University of Western Ontario Law School (1971). He took up writing novels as a retirement hobby.

Always a proponent of quantity over quality, Donald has churned out more than 100 novels since his retirement. Please check out Donald's Author Page on Amazon to find details about each book.

OTHER BOOKS BY THIS AUTHOR

SLIMY LAWYER SERIES

SLIMY LAWYER (#1 in Series)
SLIMY SUES AMERICA (#2 in Series)
SLIMY GETS SHAFTED (#3 in Series)
SLIMY GETS DISBARRED (#4 in Series)
SLIMY TASTES THE GOOD LIFE (#5 in Series)
SLIMY LAWYER CHECKS OUT (#6 in Series)

WEIRD LAWYER SERIES

WEIRD LAWYER #1 (Novice Attorney)
WEIRD LAWYER #2 (Tough Times)
WEIRD LAWYER #3 (A Pinch of Jealousy)

VANISHING LAWYER SERIES

VANISHING LAWYER #1 (A World Without Me)
VANISHING LAWYER #2 (Unwanted Witness)
VANISHING LAWYER #3 (Fugitive Alien)
VANISHING LAWYER #4 (Saving the President)
VANISHING LAWYER #5 (Swindling Seniors)
VANISHING LAWYER #6 (Saving Trump Again)

SARCASTIC LAWYER SERIES

THE WRONG LAWYER (#1 in Series)
SNARKY LAWYERS (#2 in Series)

OTHER LAWYER NOVELS

CARJACKED LAWYER (A Travel Nightmare)
LAWYER HEAVEN
REVILED LAWYER
FEISTY OLD LAWYERS (Biting Bureaucracy)
THE LAWYER WHO HATED MONEY (A Cozy Mystery)
STUBBORN LAWYER (A Canadian Mystery)
DISCARDED LAWYER (But Not Dead Yet)
LOCKDOWN LAWYER
SHUT THAT LAWYER UP
THE LORD SNATCHES AWAY
LOATHING THE LAWYER, LOVING THE LAWYER
LADY LUCK LOVES LAWYERS
LUCKY LAWYER
PARADE OF DEAD LAWYERS
THE LAWYER'S MUSLIM NEIGHBORS
REVENGE DELAYED
TERRORIST LAWYER
LAWYER IN THE TOILET

BUYING REDEMPTION
THE CHEAPSKATE TWINS
NAÏVE LAWYER
FAKE LAWYER
TEMPTING THE GOOD LAWYER
THE LIPPY LAWYER'S ROMANCE
BROKE, DISGRACED AND ALONE (A Romance)
RICH LAWYER, POOR PRIEST
LOVE SEDUCES A FOOL
A RETIRED LAWYER'S DOOMED ROMANCE

CHRISTMAS NOVELS

JOBLESS CHRISTMAS (A Travel Romance)
THE CHRISTMAS LAWYER
THE LEFT TACKLE'S CHRISTMAS

ROMANCE NOVELS

THE LAWYER AND THE PRINCESS
BEVY OF BEAUTIES (Finding Love After Loss)
SWEET ROMANCE BACK HOME

SCIENCE FICTION/SUPERNATURAL NOVELS

ALIEN SPECTATORS
FAILED LAWYER, POMPOUS ANGEL
DIVERGENT LAWYER

HAUNTED FUNERAL HOME SERIES

HAUNTED FUNERAL HOME #1 (Gorgeous Ghost)
HAUNTED FUNERAL HOME #2 (Ghost Detectives)

UNDERCOVER HILLBILLY MYSTERY/ACTION SERIES

UNDERCOVER HILLBILLY #1 (A Financial Mystery)
UNDERCOVER HILLBILLY #2 (Murder Suspect)
UNDERCOVER HILLBILLY #3 (A Stinking Mystery)

UNDERCOVER HILLBILLY #4 (Another Strange Mystery)
UNDERCOVER HILLBILLY #5 (Missing Half-Brother)
UNDERCOVER HILLBILLY #6 (Dangerous Adversary)

TY WARD ADVENTURE SERIES

TY WARD HITS AMERICA (#1 in Series)
TY WARD'S HOLIDAY FROM HELL (#2 in Series)
TY WARD'S NEXT WAR (#3 in Series)
DEADLY WITNESS (#4 in Series)
A YOUNG HOOKER'S THANKS (#5 in Series)
TY WARD'S LAST WAR (#6 in Series)
TY WARD'S SHATTERED PEACE (#7 in Series)
TY WARD'S ROUGH JUSTICE (#8 in Series)
TY WARD'S LOCKDOWN RESCUE (#9 in Series)

WARD JONES ACTION SERIES

WARD JONES #1 (Fledgling Predator)
WARD JONES #2 (Damsels in Distress)

OTHER ACTION NOVELS

STARTING OVER (Danger in Missouri)
LADY INJUSTICE (Falsely Accused)
UNQUALIFIED DETECTIVE (A Financial Mystery)
TRAILER PARK REVENGE (Crime Thriller)
VILE FAMILIES
CROSSING A RICH MAN (Turning the Tables)
ESCAPE FROM EVERYTHING (Back from War)
MARTY MARCOTTE'S REVOLVING LIFE
FIFTY YEARS LATER (Hitchhiking in Donald Trump's America)

YOUNG ADULT NOVELS

YOUNG BUT NOT STUPID
CELESTIAL COINCIDENCE

MYSTERY OF THE OLD DESK

www.ingramcontent.com/pod-product-compliance
Lightning Source LLC
Chambersburg PA
CBHW071718140626
46557CB00012B/958